RANSOM

The British Ambassador to a Scandinavian country is kidnapped and a 'planeload of innocent people hi-jacked at its airport and held to ransom for the release of a group of dangerous, convicted terrorists. Behind it is one man—Shepherd, sought by every policeman in Europe. This time it looks as if they are going to get him.

For although Shepherd holds all the cards, there is one ace stacked against him—a dogged, unassuming Scandinavian policeman who just does not know how to give up . . .

PAUL WHEELER

Ransom

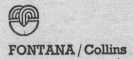

FONTANA / Collins

First published by Fontana Books 1975

© British Lion Films Limited 1975

Made and printed in Great Britain by
William Collins Sons & Co Ltd Glasgow

CHAPTER ONE

Few masks are pleasant to look upon and the one facing Barnes was no exception. It represented no one in particular; a face with a bland, almost naive expression. Had he seen such a face in real life he wouldn't have given it a second glance. Transferred on to *papier mâché*, however, with two round holes cut out for the eyes and a letter-box rectangle for the mouth, there was something compelling about it. Hypnotic was the word Barnes thought of.

The contours of the mask reached above the wearer's hairline and well below his chin. The eye recesses revealed nothing and the hole for the mouth, which had been made wider to allow the speaker more freedom, showed only a pair of quite ordinary lips. The wearer sat bolt upright behind the table, hardly moving and Barnes would have found it difficult to lean sideways to try and see what colour hair was behind the mask. Had he wished to, that is. As he sat across the table, noting down the man's demands in shaky handwriting, his brain contained a babel of voices all of which were saying 'For God's sake, don't stare! Don't upset him, keep him calm, act normal, don't even cough!'

The man in the mask waited until Barnes finished scribbling down his last words, then resumed:

'Charges against all of them will be dropped and they will be released from custody. Immediately.'

Another pause. Barnes tried to look composed, relaxed, as if he were at a talk on military strategy back in a lecture room at Sandhurst, but it was hard thinking himself into the part. They hadn't taught him this kind of warfare. They had made him an expert in spotting the high ground, providing covering fire for a platoon, at rendezvous routines beneath bushy-topped trees –

5

but not this. Who could have prophesied, ten years ago, that future wars would be conducted by quietly spoken young men with cultured accents ? Who wore conservative civilian clothes and uttered their demands in the precise, authoritative manner of a barrister ? Who wore masks and methodically crossed off a list in front of them as if they were shopping ?

Barnes nodded to indicate he had caught up. His chief anxiety was wondering how he could wipe the sweat from his pen without being noticed. He was finding it impossible to hold.

The controlled, expressionless voice continued:

'Their passports will be restored and they will be permitted to leave England at once. When these conditions have been fulfilled, I shall demand – '

A short, considerate pause as the eyes behind the mask watched Barnes's pen skim quickly over the paper, then:

' – five parachutes, transport to the airfield and an aircraft to effect our exit from this country.'

Barnes nodded. Nothing unexpected here. For a brief moment he was comforted by the thought that since the man was educated, articulate, possessed a trained mind which betrayed Oxbridge influences, all would be well. Like most Englishmen, he confused bleeding with compassion. Unlike most Englishmen, he rid himself of this confusion forever when he heard the same ordered tones add, 'Please inform the authorities that if they refuse to satisfy these demands, I shall execute one of the hostages.'

'He'll do it,' Barnes thought as he completed his notes. 'He's not bluffing, he'll do it without even thinking about it.'

His teeming thoughts slowed down his rate of writing. The man in the mask waited, the pencil between his fingers tapping the side of the table. Tickety-tick-tick-tick, tickety-tick-tick-tick. A military tattoo.

Without realising it, Barnes was writing down everything: '. . . will execute one of the hostages.' When he became aware how unnecessary it was to make a note of something he was never likely to forget, he decided to finish the sentence nevertheless.

The pencil, fluttering between the fingers of the other man, rattled against the edge of the table impatiently. Suddenly it fell on to the expensive Persian carpet.

The mask went down with the wearer's head as he bent to retrieve the pencil from the floor. As it bobbed back up again, the side caught against the edge of the table. The elastic band holding it in place stretched and then snapped.

The mask slipped sideways, dropping into the man's lap and Barnes stared into a young face, under thirty years of age. It was long, topped by fair, wavy hair and contained two deep set eyes beneath prominent eyebrows. The expression caught was one of surprise, annoyance. With a hint of fear. This last emotion was emphasised by the way the man grabbed the mask and rammed it back over his face.

For some seconds he remained silent. Then he said:

'I have three colleagues with me. We are all armed and highly trained in the use of our weapons.'

'I want to see the hostages,' Barnes said, standing.

The man thought for a moment, one hand pressing the mask to his face. Then he nodded curtly. 'Very well.'

He stood and led Barnes to a corner of the lavish, beautifully furnished room where a curtain had been improvised, shutting off an extension. Pulling the curtain to one side he nodded to Barnes who looked through the gap.

Gerald Palmer, the British Ambassador to Nordland sat in a Louis Quatorze chair. Two belts, joined at the buckles, ran round it and his body and were tied at the back. Palmer nodded:

'Hello, Frank,' he said, his voice not much above a whisper.

'Are you all right, sir?' Barnes asked. He took a step forward but the man holding the curtain stuck out a hand. 'I brought your pills.'

Barnes reached into a pocket and took out a small phial.

'His Excellency has a heart condition – ' he began to say before the man at the curtain cut him off.

7

'I am aware of that.'

'His prescription is overdue.'

'Leave them. I will see to it,' the man said.

Behind Palmer, seated next to each other on a settee were an elderly couple. Their wrists were bound together. Watching them, astride a chair back to front, sat a figure wearing a stocking mask and holding a Walther PPK .38. The tight nylon distorted the features weirdly and the terror such a vision inspired was well displayed on the faces of the two housekeepers.

The man dropped the curtain. Barnes backed off, handing him Palmer's pills.

'Every four hours without fail,' Barnes said, nodding to the phial.

The man pointed to the door. The interview was over. Barnes moved out of the living room into the hallway. Two more men, each dressed in black sweaters, each wearing stockings over their heads, each carrying powerful Smith & Wesson Magnum .357 revolvers, stood on either side of the main door. One of them leaned across, grasped the door handle and swung it inwards, staying well out of sight.

Barnes stepped outside. The sub-zero morning air gave his flushed cheeks a stinging slap as the door slammed shut behind him.

CHAPTER TWO

His wife had just opened the kitchen window and called out that lunch would be on the table in three minutes. Needing no further excuse to leave the warm drizzle of an English January he slung the fork and spade uncleaned into the garden shed and walked across the lawn to the house.

Halfway across he heard the telephone ring. By the time he reached the back door and jemmied one boot off with the toe of another his wife came through from the hall.

'It's for you,' she said. 'Someone calling from Nordland.'

Nordland? That wasn't his.

'You might tell them to find some other time to call than Sunday lunch,' his wife added. She checked the roast through the glass door of the oven. 'I like my beef rare.'

He padded through to the hall in his socks and picked up the receiver.

'Hello ... yes, speaking.'

He listened a few moments before alarm hit him.

'When? ... no, nothing. We haven't had the radio on, I don't know ...'

Then he stopped speaking and didn't say another word for a long time. Occasionally he nodded. His frown deepened. He watched his wife cross into the dining room carrying the roast on a platter with a look which said 'I'm not going to wait' – but he registered nothing.

Finally, he spoke into the receiver:

'You have absolutely no doubt about this ... ? All right. Where can I reach you? ...'

He snatched up a felt-tipped pen and scribbled a number.

'What's the dialling code for Nordland? ... all right, yes I've got it. Listen, there isn't much you can do until the Nordlandic government makes up its mind. I've got a pretty good

9

idea what it'll decide. However – if it's who you say it is, we might be able to do something. I'll ring you in one hour.'

He slowly replaced the receiver. Then he picked it up again and started to dial.

His wife stalked out of the dining room.

'For God's sake – ' she started but got no further.

'Shut up,' he replied.

She recognised the tone. Not brutal, without malice. Just a polite, firm order. She watched him as he waited, then said into the receiver:

'I'm using the scrambler – '

When he pressed the round white button on top of the telephone cradle, she returned to the dining room, closing the door discreetly.

Her husband groped for the hallway chair and sat down.

'You heard what happened in Nordland ? . . . which newscast ? . . . anyway, no matter. Our man has just called me . . . Barnes, Frank Barnes, he's the Military Attaché there . . . he saw the face of their leader. It's Martin Shepherd . . . He's positive and so am I. He described the face to me. It's Shepherd all right, no doubt about it. He's asked for the release of all the people rounded up last week, that's to be expected. But this is the interesting part – he wants parachutes and a 'plane to get out of Nordland. He's going to drop . . . four of them. He wants five 'chutes so he'll take the Ambassador with him. Listen, get hold of our contact. If we can find out where they are dropping, we've got him . . . I'm going to ring Charles, and tell him what I've told you. But no one else. The three of us. I'll handle the coppers, they don't need to know a thing. If anyone else comes in, there's more chance of a leak and a cock-up. Reach the contact and ring me back here.'

He replaced the receiver and sat a long while staring at the wall. Then he smiled, a confident, cheerful expression. He stood up, slapped his hands together like a schoolboy anticipating a win for the First Eleven and strode into the dining-room to begin his lunch.

CHAPTER THREE

Barnes rapped on the door and it opened almost at once. A gun barrel poked through and a voice said:

'Hands.'

Both he and the man by his side raised their arms straight and high above their heads. The door opened further, revealing nobody, and they walked through into the hall.

One of the gunmen closed the door while the other turned Barnes and his companion round and quickly searched their legs and bodies. Then he prodded them with his gun and they all moved into the living-room.

Shepherd had repaired his mask and stood by the fire, legs astride, as if he owned the place.

Barnes nodded towards the man with him:

'This is Colonel Tahlvik,' he said. 'He's in charge of national security.'

Shepherd looked at Tahlvik. Both of them were tall but Tahlvik was broader in the shoulders. A large, impassive man with a face that showed he had lived most of his life out of doors. If anything else could be read into the lines which ran round his eyes and down his cheeks, it might be obstinacy. He took down his hands before Barnes and stuck them in the pockets of his bulky civilian greatcoat. He never took his eyes off Shepherd, off the mask.

Shepherd returned his steady glare for several seconds before turning his head to Barnes who slowly lowered his hands.

'I know who he is,' he replied.

Barnes looked round the room. His first thought was that the gunmen were extraordinarily neat. He had expected empty food tins scattered over the floor, perhaps some of the exquisite furniture smashed. At least the reek of bodies; after all, they had been cooped up in a room now for nearly forty-eight hours.

He saw or smelled nothing of the sort. He felt worse himself; he hadn't removed his own clothes for two days and the skin on his face hung loose and heavy from lack of sleep. An ache across his shoulders had started the day before which now made him stoop when he stood on his feet.

The gunman behind him even laid a trail of after-shave lotion. 'Well?' Shepherd said.

'London has agreed,' Barnes answered.

The faintest of sighs was audible from the man with the gun behind.

'How is Mr Palmer?' Barnes said.

Shepherd crossed to the curtain and pulled it aside. Palmer was still in the high-backed chair, still roped to it by the two belts. Behind him on the settee the housekeepers were still guarded by the gunman who stood, his back to Barnes. The woman's head lay on the man's lap.

Palmer was slumped further down in the chair but he managed a weary smile for the two arrivals.

'Colonel Tahlvik,' he muttered.

Tahlvik nodded but said nothing.

'Have you been receiving your pills, sir?' Barnes asked.

Palmer nodded and indicated a carafe of water on the table near by with the phial next to it. 'I'm all right,' he said. 'What about my wife?'

'I've told her you are well,' Barnes said softly. 'She's worried, of course, but – '

'I've always made jokes about her piety,' Palmer said, a slow smile spreading painfully across his face. 'If she hadn't gone to church that morning, she would be here with us. Tell her the next time she goes, I'll be with her.'

Shepherd pulled down the curtain. 'London has agreed to what?' he demanded.

Barnes turned from the curtain and shrugged.

'To everything. The charges have been dropped against your people. They were released from custody and I've just heard they flew out of England for Amsterdam an hour ago.'

Shepherd held his wrist-watch high in front of his face, peering at it through an eyehole.

'We don't move from here until I am satisfied they are safe.'

Barnes nodded.

'Now what about your people?' Shepherd addressed the question directly to Tahlvik.

The colonel didn't answer. He kept his eyes on the mask but gave no sign he had even heard the question.

'They've agreed to give you everything you want,' Barnes said hurriedly. As he spoke he glanced nervously at Tahlvik. 'Give them everything they want'. The decision had triumphed after two days of bitter wrangling behind the political scenes in the Capital. Until Tahlvik was called into the discussions at the halfway stage no one had seriously advocated resistance. It had been a question of the speed of the capitulation. It was a purely British affair. There was no earthly reason why Nordland should be involved; there were, in fact, plenty of reasons why she should not. Put a foreign terrorist into one of your own prisons and no one is safe until he is released. West Germany was an example which hung on most lips. Remember the Munich Olympic Games massacre? Lufthansa never had an easy moment until the arrested Arabs were swapped for one of their 'planes.

But how quickly do we give in? Not too fast. Take a couple of days. Any longer and they might start shooting. What do London say? They'll go along. They'll release the people under arrest. No problem with the British. Very well, give it two days.

When Tahlvik arrived, summoned merely to set the wheels of the surrender in motion, the mood changed.

'With respect,' he had said, 'if you let them go, we will have another gang coming here next week, the week after and the week after that. We'll become a soft touch for anyone prepared to get what they want by these methods. And the world is full of them. You appointed me to be in charge of national security. Let these men go and our national security becomes a farce. Our laws become worthless.'

He had made his point but it failed to penetrate the armour of caution.

'Thank you, Colonel. However, you will give them everything they need and see to it they are out of the country as soon as possible . . .'

'But these men aren't in the British Embassy, they are in the Ambassador's private residence. Nordlandic soil. The housekeepers – Nordlandic citizens. It *is* our concern, it is very much our business . . .'

'That is all, Colonel Tahlvik, we won't detain you any longer . . .'

Barnes watched Tahlvik as he faced Shepherd, saw the set mouth, the cold, glittering eyes. 'Pray to God he doesn't blow it,' he thought. 'He agreed – '

Shepherd waited for Tahlvik to reply, then turned to Barnes.

'You understand the Ambassador will bale out with us. He will be at the end of a gun all the way from here to the airport and on to the 'plane. He will be left at the dropping zone. We'll tell you where that is when we are clear.'

'Yes,' Barnes said. Shepherd looked at Tahlvik.

'I trust you have convinced him we aren't bluffing.'

'He understands,' Barnes replied. Not with much conviction. He had known Tahlvik ever since his arrival in the Capital to take up the Military Attaché post three years ago. Met his family. They got on well. But at no time had he ever felt he could answer for him. As he was doing now. 'The Nordlandic government have agreed to provide five 'chutes, a military aircraft and pilot.'

'What kind?' The question came from the gunman stationed behind them.

Barnes turned.

'C 17.'

The gunman nodded and looked across at Shepherd.

'I know C 17s,' he said. Then he added, looking at Barnes, 'since Palmer will be wearing one of the 'chutes, you won't try putting a hole in them, will you?'

'No.'

'Very well,' Shepherd said, moving to the door. 'That is all.'

Barnes followed him but Tahlvik stayed where he was.

'Wait,' he said.

They all turned and looked at him. He strode to the curtain and pulled it aside.

'Stay where you are.' Shepherd spoke sharply but Tahlvik ignored him.

He pointed to the couple on the settee.

'What about them?'

'They will go up with us but remain on board,' Shepherd said. 'The pilot will bring them back.'

'No.'

Barnes bit his lip. His hands clenched in his pockets as he felt the tension tighten in the room.

Shepherd took three paces back and faced Tahlvik.

'Yes,' he said in a level, calm but firm voice.

Tahlvik dropped the edge of the curtain and moved to the door of the living room. Then he turned and fixed the mask with a cold, contemptuous expression.

'They do *not* go on board. You will release them at the airport. Otherwise you can stay here and rot.'

He brushed past the second gunman in the hall and opened the main door himself. Barnes hurried after him.

They stepped outside and stood facing the barrage of television cameras, newspaper reporters and police which formed a dense, silent semi-circle beyond the gates thirty yards away.

Barnes blew through his cheeks, a long sigh of relief. 'Well,' he murmured, 'so far, so good.'

Tahlvik began to walk towards the gates. 'You call total surrender good?'

Barnes gave a half smile, careful not to let his face be seen from the windows of the house. 'No, Nils,' he said. 'We don't surrender. *They* do.'

Tahlvik glanced quickly at him.

'What do you mean?'

They were almost at the gates and several reporters were moving forwards to question them.

'London called,' Barnes said. 'We know where they are going to bale out.'

CHAPTER FOUR

Shepherd watched the two men walk back down the path. He turned from the window and slowly took off his mask. He yawned and rubbed his face.

The gunman came through from behind the curtain and tore off the stocking mask to reveal the attractive features of a woman in her early twenties. The other two men arrived from the hall and eased the stockings from their heads.

All of them wanted to express their relief, to cheer, shout, stamp their feet, but they were both too tired and too cautious. Instead, they flopped down into chairs around the fire which was now dying in the grate.

'That colonel worries me,' the girl, Eva, said.

'Leave the worrying to me,' Shepherd replied. He turned to Terry, the aircraft expert. 'How fast does a C 17 go?'

Terry shrugged. 'Two fifty miles an hour top whack,' he replied.

Shepherd's lips moved silently as he made some rapid calculations in his head.

'Two hours and a bit to the dropping zone. Twenty minutes to drop and transfer to Chris. We should be safe inside three hours from leaving here.'

He looked at his watch. 'They won't have reached Amsterdam yet,' he said, more to himself. 'Eva, check the old couple.'

Eva slipped the mask over her head and pushed under the curtain. She moved round Palmer to the man and woman on the settee. Their hands were still tied in front of them. Eva checked the ropes. 'Not too tight?' she asked quietly. They shook their heads. Eva gave them an encouraging smile. 'Soon be over,' she said.

They gave no response. Eva moved back to the curtain. 'I wonder if I might have my pill?' Palmer asked.

She turned, looked at her watch. Palmer smiled: 'It is time. I don't intend to commit suicide at this stage in the game,' he said. She grinned and took the phial, shook out a pill.

She brought the carafe over with a glass, poured half a tumbler of water and placed the pill in Palmer's mouth, then tilted the glass to his lips. He gulped, swallowed, choked a couple of times before inclining his head.

'Thank you,' he said. Then added 'Eva'.

She grinned. 'It's a nice name, isn't it,' she said. 'I prefer it to my real one.'

She ducked under the curtain and rejoined the others. The fourth gunman, Mike, stretched and yawned. 'What do we do now?' he asked.

Shepherd glanced at the telephone on the desk in the corner. 'We wait,' he replied.

'Hey, look – ' Terry was pointing through the windows. They stood and went over, keeping their faces well away from the glass.

Coming up the path towards the main door three policemen were staggering under the weight of five parachute kits. They slithered and slipped on the packed snow. Terry hurried through to the hall. He opened the main door an inch and waited for the policemen to arrive.

'Put them down and back off,' he said, staying behind the door. The policemen dumped the parachutes and retreated quickly. Terry pulled the stocking mask over his face, reached out and hauled the kits in one by one.

He was looking them over when Shepherd came through. 'Regular airforce issue,' he said. 'No problem.'

CHAPTER FIVE

High on a ridge overlooking the besieged house Tahlvik stood by his car, his hands deep into his pockets and his chin tucked in against the biting cold which blustered and shoved its way through the massive houses situated in this opulent suburb of the Capital. He watched the police deliver the parachutes and return to the crowds around the gates. A few minutes later a black minibus ground in low gear up to the door of the ambassador's house, laboriously turned round and stopped. The engine died and silence returned to the scene, a silence accentuated by the padded effect of the snow which lay feet thick over the hilly landscape. The people around the gates looked on in the kind of dumb awe projected by spectators at a road accident.

Tahlvik's car was his own. In the back seats lay the paraphernalia of a man whose weekend in the country had been interrupted by the siege. A track suit, a pair of ski-ing boots, a tennis racket. A grubby paper carrier bag held a toy train and a pair of plimsolls for a twelve year old.

The exterior of the car showed signs of careless driving. Two wings were dented and scratchmarks along the side implied a garage or a driveway that was too narrow. It hadn't been cleaned in months. The telephone fitted under the dashboard looked out of place. A rich car's accessory slumming it.

Barnes detached himself from the crowd at the gates and climbed the hill towards Tahlvik. When he reached the car he was panting and his breath left his mouth in long thin bursts of steam. For some moments he said nothing, but looked in the same direction as Tahlvik, guessing he was not enjoying the scenes of surrender.

'I should have told you we knew about Marigold,' he said finally.

Tahlvik turned to look at him. 'About what?'

'Their code name for their dropping zone,' Barnes explained. 'I should have told you before we went in. I'm sorry.'

'No need. Had I known, I might have said something, acted in a way that would have told them you know. I *might*.'

The accented last word implied this wasn't likely.

'How did you find out?'

'British Intelligence have had a man working under cover for a couple of years,' Barnes replied. 'Inside Shepherd's group. Got quite close to him. There aren't many of them but the damage they've done in the last four, five years – Christ!'

'It only takes one man to drop an atom bomb,' Tahlvik said. 'No one needs the battalions any more.'

'Right.'

'Couldn't this contact have warned you Shepherd was coming here?'

'Apparently not. Saturday night he took off from London, nobody knew where. His mistake was using a chap they call Chris to meet them at the dropping zone. He told some others he had to leave town for the week-end, said where he was going. Our man picked it up and Intelligence put two and two together.'

'Let's hope,' Tahlvik said, 'that they don't come up with five.'

'This Chris fellow is a pilot. He took his Cessna with him. My guess is his job is to move them off as soon as they drop, get them somewhere safe.'

Tahlvik peered across the grey morning light at the house.

'Catching this man means a lot to you,' he said.

'It means everything,' Barnes replied. 'I'll show you his record some time. Oil refineries, power stations blown up. Telephone centres destroyed. Two British airports bombed. Arterial roads sabotaged, put out of action for weeks. Army barracks booby-trapped. You name it, he's done it. He's also, by the way, so far succeeded in killing twenty-five people. What would you do if you had someone like that in Nordland?'

'Arrest him.'

Barnes's laugh was short, sharp and empty of humour.

'For that we need evidence, and Shepherd doesn't leave any. Not even a parking ticket, nothing. We've tried. We've even tried planting some. We know he's planned all these jobs but we can't bloody well prove it. That is, until this one.'

'When you saw his face.'

'His one mistake,' Barnes said. 'And his last.'

Tahlvik glanced across and smiled briefly. 'If he's as good as you say he is,' he replied, 'I wouldn't count my chickens before they're hatched.'

'You can imagine what kind of reception the news had your people wanted to let him go,' Barnes grinned. 'Until we got the name of the dropping zone, there was hell to pay.'

'I can imagine,' Tahlvik said. 'What would have happened had Britain broken off diplomatic relations with Nordland? Just think – no more Christmas trees in Trafalgar Square.'

Barnes laughed and the gesture hurt. What started as a chuckle ended in a cough.

'God, I'm tired!' he said. 'Two days of this – '

The telephone under the dashboard gave a high-pitched squeak and Tahlvik leaned in and picked it up. A voice said 'They are making an international call, sir'.

'Plug me in,' Tahlvik ordered. There was a click at the other end and then the single ringing tone of a continental telephone came through amid crackling and interference. Someone picked up the distant telephone:

'Hello – ' the voice said, most of it lost in static.

'Hello,' Shepherd's voice said, more clearly, 'this is Sunflower.'

The distant voice suddenly became excited:

'Sunflower, you did it! We're out, we're here in sunny Amsterdam, can't you smell the tulips?'

'All right, let me speak to each one of you, one at a time.'

Shepherd's cautious, moderate voice contrasted greatly with the near hysterical pleasure on the other end.

Tahlvik and Barnes heard six voices, two women among them, take the telephone and give their names to Shepherd. They all called him Sunflower.

When they had all spoken Shepherd said, 'Good. Now you are on your own. I advise you to disperse. You know where to go. We are moving out now. We'll drop as arranged. Signing off.'

The telephone went dead. Tahlvik replaced the receiver on the hook.

'We've got him!' Barnes said, ramming a fist into the palm of his other hand.

'Not yet,' Tahlvik said.

'You're as cautious as Shepherd,' Barnes exclaimed. 'He's going to drop as arranged. You heard him.'

'Yes.'

The police began to move about near the gates after they also had heard the telephone call, getting ready, pushing the journalists and television cameramen back to clear a way from the entrance.

'Shepherd isn't one of your college anarchists, Nils,' Barnes added, as they began to walk down the slope towards the gates. 'He doesn't use Che Guevara just to get a hard on.'

'So don't underestimate him,' Tahlvik replied.

As they walked down the hill to the activity around the gates, a jet aircraft threaded through the leaden clouds overhead, descending to begin its run-in to the airport. Barnes had to shout to make his words carry to Tahlvik who looked up in the direction of the noise.

CHAPTER SIX

Captain Denver brought the Boeing 737 down through the last ceiling of low clouds which scudded across the airport. The crossed runways came into sight and the control tower verified permission to touch down.

'Three minutes late in weather like this,' he said to the second pilot, John Roper. 'Can't be bad.'

Roper was running his watch on an hour. Ann, the chief stewardess, put her head round the door. 'Everyone belted up and unsmoking,' she said. 'Any delays?'

'On the nose but for three minutes,' Denver replied.

'I mean getting back to London,' she said. 'There's a hell of a lot of snow down there.'

'It must be the weather,' Roper said.

'Funny,' she answered. 'I have a date at six o'clock in Leicester Square. If I don't turn up, he won't marry me.'

'Then you'll be able to stay with the airline,' Denver said. 'Loyalty to the company is going to force me to go back the long way round.'

'This thing going on in the Capital,' Roper remarked. 'I bet they've got security screwed up pretty tight. I wouldn't bet on an early take-off.'

'Oh no!' Ann groaned. 'That's bound to slow things down. I forgot about that.'

'Go and sit down,' Denver said. 'Here we go – '

The engine whine increased in pitch as the flaps opened on the wings, slowing the aircraft to bring it in line with the runway and prepare it for touchdown.

Ann moved to her seat which faced the members of First Class. A strange lot in First this trip, she thought as she pulled the seat belt across her lap. A couple of gloomy Danes and a

23

Queen's Messenger whose diplomatic pouches occupied more seats than the passengers. Thank God for the Diplomatic Service. Without their mail these offbeat routes wouldn't pay their way. Not in mid-winter and midweek. Economy was three quarters full. English ski-ing freaks who dismissed Switzerland and Austria as kids' stuff and preferred overland treks. A few lower-echelon figures from the North Sea oil business who hadn't yet been promoted to flying where the champagne was nasty but free.

Someone hadn't closed the curtain between the two compartments and Ann felt a twinge of annoyance. The two girls working for her this trip were not the best she had flown with. One had spilled tea over a passenger and blamed it on her period.

Relax, she told herself. The curtain is only important at mealtimes to stop those in steerage seeing the hot meals served to the quality while they bite on plastic beef slices. Will there be a delay going back? She had said definitely she could make the date and he wasn't the kind to be stood up, even if she said her flight had crashed.

There was a sudden flurry of activity up the gangway in the economy section. Several people were standing up. One, a young, well-built man was moving down the aisle towards her. Moving fast. Her first thought was that he was going to be sick and didn't want to do it into the bag. Trying to reach the lavatories – but they were at the rear of the cabin.

She unbuckled her belt and stood as he came through First, still moving resolutely forward.

'I'm sorry, sir,' Ann said, using the no-nonsense tone they were taught to rely on when all else failed, 'but you must remain in your seat – '

The man acted as if she weren't there. He pushed by her and moved to the door of the pilot's cockpit.

There he waited until she caught up with him. 'What do you think you're doing – ' she began but never completely finished. The man had drawn a revolver and held the profile of the gun up for her to see. Ann stared at the weapon, then at the person holding it.

'Take me in to the captain,' he whispered. 'Right this second.'

Nobody in the First Class compartment could see the gun and the man spoke so quietly that his voice was drowned by the engine noise long before it could carry to the nearest passengers.

She leaned forwards and opened the cabin door.

The man with the gun pushed her in front of him and moved into the tiny, cramped cockpit.

Beyond the windscreen the tarmac was rushing up to meet them. He leaned over and rested the barrel of the gun against Denver's neck. Denver stiffened, half turned but forced his attention back to the most dangerous time of any flight. The touch-down.

'Captain Denver,' the man said, his voice carrying a slight London accent, 'I am with three other men. Your aircraft is wired up to explode. Do exactly as I say. Come to rest on the runway farthest from the terminal buildings.'

Roper twisted round in his seat and took a hand off the controls.

'Don't!' snapped Denver. Roper froze. He looked at Denver who was staring straight ahead, his hands gently handling the stick.

The white reaches of the airfield bobbed up under the aircraft as it touched down. On first impact the gun barrel moved an inch up the nape of Denver's neck. Then the weight of the Boeing came down a second and heavier time. The man with the gun held on with his free hand. Ann, paralysed with fright since she had seen the gun, fell sideways against the side of the cockpit.

The gunman looked round quickly at her and for a second the barrel left Denver's neck. Denver reached out with his right hand and snapped two red switches upwards. Roper saw him and for an instant his eyes widened. The barrel returned to rest against Denver's skin as he jammed on all brakes.

The low-key, relaxed authority of the radio controller in the tower three hundred yards away vanished as he watched a sheet of flame shoot out from the wheels of the Boeing as it raced along the runway towards him.

'Jesus Christ!'

The other five members of the Control Tower staff looked up through the green-tinted windows. The soundproofing took away much of the drama below them but as experts they didn't need to hear anything. They watched the Boeing snake along the tarmac, still doing a hundred and ten miles an hour, on the steel rims of its wheels. All the rubber had been left in long smouldering strips fifty yards behind.

'What's happened?'

'The bloody fool's taken off his anti-skid!'

Inside the aircraft all hell was breaking loose in the passenger cabins. Coats rained down from the overhead compartments, increasing the panic of the people below who were rebounding off each other and twitching like marionettes. Bottles smashed under their feet where the duty free carriers were stored and the smell of whisky mingled with the dust shaken from the floor by the buffeting of the fuselage.

Denver held on to the stick, grappling with it like a bull wrangler. The gunman reached forward and looped an arm round his neck, prodding his gun barrel painfully against his head.

In front of them the air port landscape slipped crazily from side to side as the aircraft skidded onwards in a long meandering series of curves. Miraculously the huge machine kept going forwards. The wing flaps, reared high like the neck feathers on an angry cockerel, fought the slipstream and the speedometer needle raced backwards round the dial.

Gradually the buffeting lessened. The terminal buildings loomed up to one side. The gunman released Denver's neck but kept the feel of the gun on him.

'Away from the terminals,' he shouted. 'Move out. Out!

Denver twisted the stick and the lumbering aeroplane

trundled off the tarmac and began to jolt across the unkempt grass between the runways. The jolting was renewed fiercely as the wheel rims below bounced over the rock-hard frozen field.

Their speed dropped from forty miles an hour to ten. Denver, fighting to hold on to the controls said, 'She's stopping.'

'As far as you can,' the gunman repeated.

But the Boeing rumbled on for ten more yards then stopped. The fuselage listed some degrees before it finally came to rest.

'That's as far as she'll go.' Denver stopped. He didn't turn round. He kept his eyes straight ahead. As anyone would with a gun barrel chafing their top vertebrae.

Behind them the first sounds of panic could be heard. Weeping, shouting. People who were frightened a second ago now angry.

A second man pushed open the door of the cockpit. 'What happened?' he asked. The first gunman shrugged and pointed to the controls.

'I don't know,' he said. 'You're the expert.'

The newcomer pushed through and looked over the dashboard.

It took him ten seconds before he reached over and pressed the two red switches up and down three times.

'He took off the anti-skid,' he reported.

'Well now,' the first gunman said. 'Wasn't that smart?'

'I can't think too clearly with a gun in my neck,' Denver said quietly.

'You'd better start learning,' the gunman answered. 'And fast.'

He turned to the other. 'What's going on back there?'

'We have a problem.'

The first gunman peered through the windscreen at the distant Control Tower. Fire engines and ambulances were marshalling beneath it and they could see dozens of technicians swarming around them.

'Call in,' the gunman said, poking Denver with the barrel, 'and hold off that lot.'

He pointed to the fire trucks. He turned to go, then stopped. 'Turn round, Denver,' he said.

Denver obeyed him, twisting in his seat. The gunman held up his arm, baring a wrist watch.

'All four of us,' he said quietly, 'are wearing these.'

He handed his gun to the other man and gently picked at the winder mechanism on the watch. The spindle slid out of the works about two inches. He put a fingertip on top of the spindle.

'It takes two seconds to press in the plunger. Two seconds to send this plane a hundred feet in the air. So, tell your friends in the tower that the first whiff of gas through the air intake, any smart-alec trick like that, and we'll detonate. Is that absolutely clear?'

'Absolutely,' Denver replied.

'You'll go up with the 'plane,' Roper said.

The man retrieved his gun and stuck it into his waistband under his coat. He gave Roper a long look:

'That's right,' he said, then pushed his way out of the cockpit, followed by the second man.

Ann burst into tears.

'What do we do?' Roper said, looking at Denver.

Denver reached for his radio. 'We do exactly as he says. You know the rules. This man is a pro.'

He opened his radio link with the Tower. 'Hello Control, this is Able Charlie Six – '

The gunman moved back to where the passengers were now milling in the gangways. The second man joined two others who were vainly trying to persuade them to sit down, that everything was under control. None of them held a gun and when the first man reached out and took the aircraft intercom. telephone from the hook, his own automatic was hidden beneath his coat.

28

'Ladies and gentlemen,' he said. Then louder: 'Ladies and gentlemen!'

The panic subsided for a few moments as people looked round to find the source of the metallic voice.

'May I have your attention,' the man went on. 'The aircraft has now come to a halt and you are in no danger. I repeat you are in no danger. Please go back to your seats.'

His gentle insistence and unhurried manner produced an instant effect. Most of the passengers took him to be a member of the crew. They stood undecided for a moment. Then they realised he was telling the truth. The aircraft *had* stopped. All the jostling still continuing was being made by themselves.

'Thank you, ladies and gentlemen, thank you for your co-operation,' the man said into the telephone. 'That's fine. If you could all just sit down for a moment.'

Slowly they disentangled themselves and sat down. A silence fell throughout the cabins. The Queen's Messenger, surrounded by the hessian bags of mail, drew them closer to him but otherwise gave no indication of anything being wrong.

He turned his head and watched the man continue to speak in calm, moderate tones into the intercom.

'Despite the rocky landing,' he went on, 'the 'plane is quite safe. As I said, we are in no danger. The captain unfortunately removed the anti-skid device and as a result blew out all the tyres. This will mean quite a long repair job before the 'plane can take off again. He had a reason for doing this which I'll now explain. If you look round, you will see three men besides myself standing in the gangway.'

People turned round and saw the men standing alongside them. The men smiled down at them; cheerful, friendly grins.

'We have no alternative but to detain you on board for a short time.'

A few murmurs: 'What? . . . why, what for . . . ?'

'Let me say again,' the voice over the intercom said, 'no one is in any danger at all as long as you stay calm and in your seats. Your comfort will be fully considered and you will be kept informed of all developments. We are hopeful you will all be released within the hour. Thank you.'

He clicked off. A silence followed, broken by a low murmur, a spreading sense of confusion, as if the passengers had not quite heard every word of an announcement.

'What did he say . . . why do we have to stay on board . . . maybe they can't get the doors open. . . . It's probably where we've ended up. The snow's thick outside, they have to get special trucks to reach us . . .'

The gunman replaced the telephone, smiled quickly to himself and turned back towards the pilot's cabin.

Only one person in the Economy section could say anything definite. A ruddy-faced, portly man who looked exactly what he was. Major Ferris R.E. (Retd). 'Bloody hell!' Ferris exclaimed. 'We've been hi-jacked!'

As the gunman came into the pilot's cabin, Denver was still talking to Control.

The ambulances and rescue trucks were now stopped on the edge of the tarmac a hundred yards away. Denver looked round as the gunman said, 'Let me talk to them.'

'Stand by, Control,' Denver said and passed over the microphone.

The gunman took it.

'Hello, Control. I want you to connect me with telephone number 729523. No questions, no debates. Do it.'

He handed the microphone back to Denver, crossed his arms in a patiently waiting gesture, smiled briefly at both pilots and leaned against the side of the cockpit.

CHAPTER SEVEN

The main door of the Ambassador's house had been opened for five minutes before Tahlvik and Barnes saw one of the men come out hauling two of the parachute kits. He moved to the minibus, opened the rear doors and threw them in. Then he returned inside and a few seconds later dragged out the other three. The driver of the minibus remained motionless in the driving seat while this was going on.

Beyond the gates a path had been cleared to allow the vehicle to pass through the waiting crowds and police were keeping control of the journalists who jostled each other, anticipating action.

Barnes spoke once or twice to Tahlvik as they stood on the ridge looking down at the scene but got no reply. It wasn't hard to guess Tahlvik's thoughts as he stared impassively at the preparations for the evacuation of the house. Barnes decided wisely to abandon any further attempt to sugar the pill the colonel was trying to swallow and stayed silent.

Inside the house Eva was helping the housekeeper couple gently to their feet. The woman gave a cry of pain as she stood up and fell heavily back on to the settee. The man bent and spoke to her. She pointed to the calves of her legs and he carefully kneaded them to restore the circulation. It was hard going with his wrists bound but he didn't ask for them to be untied.

Shepherd brought the mask down over his face and lifted the curtain.

'All right,' he said, 'we're moving out.'

He stopped when he saw the woman lying down, her face twisted with pain and the man massaging her legs.

'Cramp,' Eva said.

'We have to go. Now!' Shepherd said. 'Support her.'

Eva tucked her gun into her belt and bent to lift the woman to her feet. The man took one arm, she took the other but it was difficult with her hands tied. Shepherd watched them for a moment before coming forward. He took a penknife from a pocket and slit through the cord tying the woman's wrists.

'Now get a move on,' he said to Eva.

Palmer was already standing. 'Can you walk?' Shepherd asked him.

'I'm all right,' the Ambassador replied. 'I wouldn't like to forget my pills, however.'

Shepherd picked up the phial and put it into Palmer's trouser pocket.

'Where do you keep your topcoat?' Shepherd asked.

'Upstairs in the bedroom wardrobe.'

Shepherd sent Mike to look for warm clothing for Palmer while Eva helped the elderly couple to move through to the hall.

'We get into the minibus,' he told them. 'I'll be with Palmer in the rear seats. Terry in front with the driver, Mike, Eva and the housekeepers behind.'

Mike came down the stairs carrying a bulky Nordlandic fur coat. He handed it to Palmer who looked at his wrists which were bound.

'We have a problem,' he said.

'No you don't,' Shepherd replied. He took the coat, drew it round Palmer's shoulders and buttoned it in front, keeping his arms pinioned underneath.

'Terry, you first,' Shepherd went on. 'Up into the passenger seat. Keep your gun in the driver's ribs. You never know. He could be a policeman or a soldier. Search him.'

Terry nodded and stood by the door for a moment. Inside the living room the telephone rang. Shepherd snapped his head round in surprise. Terry dodged out through the door and clambered quickly up beside the driver. The telephone continued to ring.

'Wait here,' Shepherd said and hurried back to pick up the receiver.

'Yes – ?'

A crackling erupted through the earpiece then a voice came across the wire, urgent, excited: 'Sunflower, hello, Sunflower ?'

'This is Sunflower – '

'Sunflower, this is Petrie, I repeat, this is Petrie – '

'What – ? Where are you – ?'

'At the airport. Listen carefully. Marigold is blown! Do not move out of the house. Marigold is blown. Do you read me ?'

'But how ?' For the first time a note of panic tinged Shepherd's voice.

'The pigs have got Chris! He radioed me from Marigold! They must have followed him, I don't know how but they found out where you are dropping! He called through to say they were closing in. They're swarming all over the place waiting for you!'

Shepherd went silent for a moment. His brain raced over the preparations made during the past few weeks. How did they get on to Chris ? Who talked ?

'Listen, Sunflower,' Petrie's voice came back on the line, 'we've hijacked a 'plane. We're here at the airport. We've got seventy or eighty people on board. We'll get you out. Just sit tight. Do you read me, Sunflower ?'

A slight pause before Shepherd answered: 'I read you Ray. Good luck.'

'Stand by. I'll get back to you. Good luck, Sunflower.'

The line went dead. Shepherd stood for a second with the receiver in his hand. Then he slammed it down and ran back into the hall. The others had heard his end of the telephone call and guessed things had gone wrong.

'Get Terry,' he snapped. 'Everyone back in here. Hurry!'

He led the way back into the living-room and stood by the dead fire looking into the ashes. His fingers betrayed the feeling of uncertainty which now took hold of him. Up until a minute ago he had been fully in command. The plan had worked to the letter. Everything they had calculated had turned out as they expected. The Nordlanders said they could go, the Brits released the people under arrest – and now this. He traced the outline of the mantelpiece with a restless hand as he tried to bring the next few hours into focus. Petrie was a good man. He had almost dealt him in on this operation but in the end they needed a radio man and someone clued in to aeroplanes. As it turned out, leaving Petrie behind was just as well. There weren't many in the group who'd calmly commandeer a civil aircraft at a moment's notice. Petrie was the only consolation he had, but it was insufficient to compensate for his loss of command. Now they were all in the hands of somebody else. Somebody they couldn't even contact. He hoped he was right about Petrie's potential.

Palmer and the housekeepers returned and Shepherd nodded to the curtain. Eva, Mike and Terry led them into the closed-off part of the room and sat them down in the chairs they occupied earlier. Terry passed the belts around Palmer and secured them at the back of the Louis Quatorze chair. Eva retied the woman's hands but left the cord reasonably slack. No one spoke. They were well-trained and none showed the fear they all felt deep in their stomachs. When the hostages were settled they left them and pulled the curtain across.

They pulled off their masks and stood watching Shepherd. There was a long silence before he turned to them. He slipped off his mask and they could see the worry on his face.

'The police discovered where we were to drop. They're there now, waiting for us.'

'What happened?' Eva asked.

'It appears they got on to Chris.'

'That's ridiculous!' Terry exclaimed.

'Yes,' Shepherd nodded, 'it is. However, it's also a fact.'

'Some idiot talked,' Mike said.

Shepherd gave a thin smile. 'Five people knew about Marigold,' he said quietly. 'We four – and Chris. Anybody here say anything?'

34

Silence.

'Very well,' he went on. 'The police got wind of the drop zone, or they followed Chris, or Chris told them.'

'I can't believe he would do that,' Terry said. He felt involved in the failure; it had been he who had brought Chris into the group. They had flown together in Africa and Bangladesh. He could vouch for him. If someone had got through to the police, it wasn't Chris.

'That's why they've all been so bloody co-operative,' Mike said. 'The 'chutes, the 'plane out of here. Letting the others out of jail – '

Shepherd broke in quickly, his voice sharp and reproving. 'I don't care to waste time on post-mortems,' he said. 'We'll think only of the present situation. We are here. We can't get out under our own steam. Ray Petrie has hi-jacked a 'plane and is standing right now at the airport. Very well. We have no choice but to wait for him. I see no reason why we won't be let out. We now have a hundred hostages instead of three. They were letting us leave five minutes ago. They have a far more compelling reason now to do the same thing.'

'We could still go to the airport,' Eva remarked. 'We've got the Ambassador. They wouldn't stop us.'

'True,' Shepherd said. 'But we do nothing until Petrie comes through again. Meanwhile disperse around the house. We need all round vision. They could make some move. Try and catch us while we're disoriented. Spread out.'

His calm, firm orders brought the necessary results and the other three shook off the defeat that had suddenly fallen round their shoulders and took off into various parts of the house to stand guard.

Shepherd remained in the living room. He didn't move from the hearth and his eyes hardly blinked as he looked down at the grate. 'Now it starts to get difficult.'

The voice came from behind the curtain. Shepherd turned his head but made no reply.

'You've lost the initiative,' Palmer went on. 'You have to rely on somebody else.'

'That isn't difficult,' Shepherd replied.

'You don't think so?'

'Not if you trust them.'

'Ah, but *do* you trust them?' Palmer said. 'With your money, yes. With minor things. But today you're trusting them with your life. When you make that kind of commitment you'd be surprised how differently you regard people.'

Shepherd stayed silent. A quiet chuckle erupted from the curtain.

'Forgive me for saying so,' Palmer said, 'but you have struck me as a man who finds it hard to delegate authority.'

This time Shepherd's face creased into a tight smile. 'Well,' he said, 'now appears to be the perfect time to learn.'

'Waiting,' Palmer said after a pause. 'That's the worst part.'

'We've waited two days,' Shepherd answered. 'We weathered that.'

'But then your fate was in your own hands. Now it rests in the hands of someone called Petrie. It rests with someone whom you can't even contact. If he makes one mistake my friend, you are dead.'

'*We* are dead, my friend,' Shepherd said.

On the other side of the curtain Palmer heard the last words. He grinned quickly, glancing behind him at the elderly couple. The man nodded back and Palmer gave him a look to convey, as best he could, some sort of optimism.

CHAPTER EIGHT

Tahlvik and Barnes saw a second masked gunman run out of the house and speak to the first who had climbed into the minibus beside the driver. They watched the two of them sprint back inside the house and slam the door.

Barnes was saying 'What the hell's going on?' when Tahlvik's telephone buzzed. 'Tahlvik.'

'Shepherd just took a call from the airport, Colonel,' a voice said. 'Something's gone wrong. The person on the line was calling from an aircraft he claims to have hi-jacked at the airport. Apparently the British police have discovered where Shepherd and his men were planning to bale out. The hi-jackers told Shepherd this, told him to stay where he is.'

'The 'plane's on the ground?' Tahlvik asked.

'I presume so. We can't be sure. We monitored the 'phone call, that's all. We haven't called the airport. I didn't have time to plug you in to listen. I'm sorry, Colonel.'

'What else was said?'

'Nothing, sir. Oh, yes. The hi-jacker's name. Petrie. Ray Petrie.'

Tahlvik slammed the receiver back on to the hook under the dash. Barnes was looking at him askance.

'We now have a hi-jack on our hands,' Tahlvik said, thinking about something else. He spoke into the telephone. 'The airport and fast.'

'A hi-jack?' Barnes repeated, frowning.

'It looks like someone leaked the fact you know their dropping zone,' Tahlvik said as he waited, holding the receiver. 'Who do you know with a big mouth?'

'How could they have found out we knew –' Barnes began, his face reddening. Then a voice came through on the telephone.

'This is Colonel Tahlvik,' Tahlvik began. The voice spoke quickly and he listened for almost half a minute. Finally he said:

'I will be there in twenty minutes. Don't give them anything until I arrive. Meanwhile, I want to know where the flight originated. . . . London ? Any stopovers ? . . . well, check. Also, how many passengers are on board. We have one name so far, Ray Petrie. Ask London to telex through a flight list. It's probably a false name but we have to start right at the bottom.'

He replaced the telephone.

'Of all the luck!' Barnes said.

'I'm going to need some help, Frank,' Tahlvik said. 'Is there anything in your diplomatic protocol that prevents you lending me a hand ?'

'Probably,' Barnes replied with a smile. 'But I'll ignore it.'

Tahlvik nodded to the car seat beside him and Barnes moved round the car and climbed in. Tahlvik released the brake and they rolled down the slope to the crowds round the gates who were talking among themselves, frowning and unsure what had happened. Tahlvik called over a police inspector. Briefly he described what had just occurred at the airport.

'Tell the Press,' Tahlvik said, 'but I'd be grateful if you'd take your time. I'd like a head start to the airport. If those boys start off in their fast cars, I won't be able to move for the traffic.'

The inspector saluted and said he would tell them in ten minutes. Tahlvik drove away, picking up speed as soon as he could to shrug off any inquisitive reporter who might wonder why and where they were going.

Soon they were driving fast along the ribbon of road that stretched through the unbroken whiteness of the deep snow lying over the silent landscape. Neither of them spoke for ten minutes. Barnes looked round behind them and saw the track suit, the plimsolls and the tennis racket.

'Where were you when this started ?' he asked.

'Up at the lodge,' Tahlvik replied.

Barnes touched the track suit. 'You actually run outside in this weather ?' he asked incredulously.

'We are winter people,' Tahlvik replied. 'We only come alive when the snow falls. We are uncomfortable in the summertime. We are self-conscious in a bathing suit. There is nothing wrong with running in the snow. It is the perfect way to improve the circulation.'

A car approached them from behind and gave a long blast on the horn followed by several short ones. Barnes turned round while Tahlvik looked in the driving mirror.

'Who is this idiot – ?' he started to say when the car, a huge black saloon, pulled out and overtook them. Then it slewed across the road in front, dropping its nose into a soft pile of banked snow by the kerb. Tahlvik heaved on the wheel and hit the brakes hard.

'The bloody fool!' he yelled as the car went into an S-shaped skid out of control. It looked inevitable they would sideswipe the black car, which had now stopped, but Tahlvik pumped the brake, reduced the skidding and finally screeched to a halt a yard from the body of the car in front.

He was out in a second and striding angrily over to the black saloon.

Two men got out the back. One of them was a man of about sixty, a squat, solid body surmounted by a massive head. He turned round and Tahlvik checked his pace when he recognised General Olaf Polson, the senior serving officer at the Defence ministry. The man with him was tall and thin, wearing a neatly cut topcoat, pinched in at the waist. Apart from a white shirt, every other piece of clothing on his body was black. Bureaucracy black.

'General Polson – ' Tahlvik said.

'Tahlvik, thank God we caught you.'

'You almost killed me,' Tahlvik said, his voice retaining an angry tone even if some of the invective he had planned was sent back before delivery.

'That was Bernhard's idea,' Polson said, pointing to the front car. 'It's a government car. He doesn't have to pay for the repairs. Do you, Bernhard?'

It didn't take extra sensory perception to detect a strong dislike between Tahlvik and Bernhard. Probably born of many previous meetings where negotiations were carried on amid a prevailing mood of mutual contempt. Among civilian Government circles, the army was regarded at best as a joke, at worst an unnecessary burden upon the taxpayer. Bernhard didn't invent this fashionable view but he believed in it. Tahlvik had no particular grudge against Bernhard, but the man was the right arm to the Ministry of the Interior. He had a seat in Parliament and a long record of anti-military speeches and represented a direct threat to the continued existence of all the armed forces.

'You are going to the airport?' Bernhard inquired.

'Yes.'

'You are acquainted with their demands?'

'No.'

'The hi-jackers will exchange the passengers for their friends at present inside the house of the British Ambassador. It is the Government's view that we yield to their demands.'

'The Government certainly made up its mind quickly,' Tahlvik said. 'The hi-jack took place less than thirty minutes ago.'

'No time is to be lost over this affair,' Bernhard said.

'You took two days making up your minds over their friends. Oh, and it was the Government's view we released them as well, wasn't it?'

'I see no point standing here discussing the matter,' Bernhard said. He looked everywhere but directly into Tahlvik's eyes. He seemed more concerned with the distant skyline, peering across the snowed fields through half-closed lids.

Tahlvik looked at Polson. 'I've said this before but it bears repetition,' he said. 'If we give in now, we'll have another hi-jack next week and the week after. We'll never be free of them.'

'If we try to resist, Tahlvik,' Bernhard said, 'a hundred innocent people might well be blown to pieces. We cannot justify such a massacre. In a situation like this the Government is powerless.'

He glanced at Polson who didn't appear to be listening.

'Oh, I entirely agree,' the General said, shaking his heavy head. 'And we mustn't forget another important fact.'

'What is that, sir ?' Tahlvik asked.

'There's an election coming up. I can't see the Government wanting to run on a programme that includes a readiness to commit mass murder. Eh, Bernhard ?'

Bernhard nodded curtly. He was never sure if Polson was mocking him or not.

'Should that aircraft explode,' he said, 'history will never forget that we were the first country in the world to sacrifice the passengers rather than yield to the pirates.'

'I'm not saying we sacrifice them,' Tahlvik said. 'I'm saying we should at least try and explore the possibilities of getting them off without giving in.'

'This isn't a war game, Colonel,' Bernhard remarked. 'There isn't what you people call "an acceptable level of casualties".'

Tahlvik opened his mouth to retaliate, his brow dropping in anger, but Polson intervened. 'Absolutely right, Bernhard,' he said. He returned Tahlvik's glare of stunned astonishment with a mild glance, accompanied by the merest of shrugs.

Bernhard turned his head and looked across at Tahlvik's car. 'Is that Captain Barnes with you ?' he asked.

Tahlvik nodded. 'Yes.'

Bernhard walked over to speak to Barnes who had remained inside the car.

As he left Polson took Tahlvik's arm and led him a few yards in the opposite direction.

'Sir – ' Tahlvik spoke under his breath and kept his face concealed from Bernhard's direction.

'Politicians and civil servants hate to be argued with,' Polson said. 'I never do it. As a result they do exactly what I want them to do. Now pay attention. The Ambassador was a British affair. This hi-jack is ours. Here are your orders. You will delay giving into them. You'll endeavour to get the gunmen off the aircraft. In doing so, you will not endanger the life of a single passenger. Is that clear, Tahlvik?'

'Perfectly clear, General,' he replied. 'Clear and quite impossible.'

'Excellent,' Polson grinned. 'We understand each other.'

Tahlvik's face relaxed a fraction as the older man patted his arm and turned to walk back to Bernhard who was returning from Barnes to his car.

'I have a strong aversion to a bunch of foreign anarchists holding the country to ransom,' Polson muttered as they drew nearer to Bernhard.

Tahlvik looked across at the civil servant. 'What about him?'

'Try diplomacy. If that fails – .'

'Use force?' Tahlvik said, lifting an eyebrow.

'Improvise,' Polson said, leaving the subject of force an open alternative.

'You will bear in mind, Colonel Tahlvik,' Bernhard said, 'there are women and children on board that 'plane.'

He summoned Polson to follow him to his car where the chauffeur started the engine. As Polson followed he turned: 'Don't forget that, Tahlvik,' he called. 'Women and children.'

They climbed into their car and the chauffeur eased the radiator from the snowbank. It scraped round in a fast U-turn and raced away, the fumes from the exhaust creating a long blossoming trail of steam in the crisp, caustic air.

'Did Bernhard give you a hard time?' Barnes asked as Tahlvik returned to the wheel.

'I don't know,' Tahlvik replied. 'I wasn't listening.'

They drove on towards the airport. Tahlvik returned to the telephone and spoke to the Control Tower to ask what was happening. They were in the middle of telling him when the car entered a tunnel as the road pierced a hill and all communication was drowned in a sea of interference. The tunnel was about two hundred yards long and curved gently round so that for half the distance they were driving in total darkness.

Tahlvik held the receiver with one hand and the wheel with the other. 'What was Bernhard saying to you back there?' he asked.

Barnes grinned. 'I'm not sure, but I think he was reminding me of the duties of a foreign military attaché,' he said.

'You mean, keep out of it.'

'He's not terribly keen on the army, is he?'

'British understatement making its point again,' Tahlvik grunted. 'He hates us.'

'Why?'

'I think it has something to do with winning votes. His party will soon be fighting at the polls. The party who promises to cut defence and reduce the armed services is usually the party that wins. It's become a tradition. That's why he'll try and make it look as if we are mishandling this business.'

'What did he say?' Barnes asked.

'He said we should yield.'

'What are you going to do?'

'I'm not sure yet,' Tahlvik said as they came out of the end of the tunnel into the light. 'You can't fight a battle without looking at the battle-ground.'

He brought the telephone back to his ear.

'Hello, Control? We went through a tunnel. Can you repeat what the present position is? Has anything been said to the hi-jackers from the tower?'

CHAPTER NINE

The passengers were quiet as Petrie wandered up the aisle to have brief words with Joe, Bert and Pete who stood at intervals up the fuselage. They told him things were cool. Most of the passengers were now aware the delay was not a technical one and they cast sideways glances at the four standing men, afraid of the immediate future. However, since none of the hi-jackers were showing their guns and Petrie had the other three acting as *ad hoc* stewards for some of the older members of the Economy section, or offering to bring milk to the two babies on board, the edge of the drama was blunted.

Except where Major Ferris was concerned. Seated behind him were two Japanese businessmen who were perhaps the only two in the aircraft who still had no idea what was happening. They spoke only Japanese and, therefore, only to each other. Twice one tried to stand but was politely pushed down into his seat by Bert. The same man spoke to Bert but the language barrier was insurmountable.

'Yeah, sure, love,' Bert told him. 'Now just sit there and sukiyaki your sayonara, Okay?'

Ferris glowered at Bert and when he moved away some yards, leaned over to the man seated next to him. 'Isn't anyone going to do anything?' he whispered.

His neighbour looked at him, alarmed. 'Like what?'

'Good God man!', Ferris exclaimed. 'Are we just going to sit here and let these hooligans tell us what to do?'

'I am,' his neighbour said flatly. 'And if you have any sense at all, you will too.'

The warning was lost on Ferris who could scarcely contain his irritation. Long-haired yobboes telling him to sit down and be quiet? A man who had been through the desert campaign and was mentioned in despatches – ?

He turned round and spoke softly through the space between the seats to the Japanese behind:

'Hey! Hey, you – ' Ferris hissed. He checked Bert was not looking and bobbed up to peer over the back of his seat.

The Japs looked up apprehensively.

'Are you on to have a go?' Ferris said under his breath.

He watched them stare at him.

'Have – a – go?' he repeated.

One of the men said something to his friend. Then they both returned to looking up at Ferris with blank expressions.

Ferris slid down into his seat. 'What the devil's the matter with everyone?' he muttered.

'I think they want to stay alive,' said his neighbour.

Ferris looked up the aisle behind him.

Bert had now moved to the back of the aircraft, standing by the lavatories. He was leaning over and tweaking the ears of a large Snoopy doll seated between a boy of about four and his mother. The boy was grinning and talking happily to Bert, despite his mother's frightened gestures. She put a hand on his arm and told him to be quiet. The boy ignored her and began to show Bert how a zip opened up the belly of the doll. Inside was a collection of toy cars. Bert picked one up and examined it admiringly while the boy showed him his favourite, an Aston Martin.

'He's got expensive tastes, hasn't he?' Bert said to the mother, who nodded quickly and looked out through the window.

Ferris stood up. 'Whare are you going?' said his neighbour.

'Mind your own damned business,' Ferris said, pushing past.

'If you are going to encourage them to start shooting, it *is* my damned business,' the man replied.

Ferris stood in the aisle. Pete came up to him. 'What's your problem, matey?'

'I'd – er – I'd like to pay a call,' Ferris murmured, pointing to the lavatories.

Pete considered the request a second then shrugged. 'O.K.'

Ferris strolled up the aisle, trying hard to look casual. He approached Bert and pointed again to the lavatories behind, muttering something incoherent. Bert eased to one side to let him pass, continuing to admire the boy's model car collection.

Ferris shoved open the door of one of the lavatories and closed it behind him.

A second later he re-opened it a fraction. He peered through at Bert's back, still bent as he leaned over the boy's seat.

Ferris waited five seconds, then opened the door silently and hurled himself on top of Bert.

His impetus shoved Bert down almost squashing the boy. Ferris ran an arm round his neck and heaved backwards. Both of them fell to the floor and people turned and screamed as they saw Bert draw an automatic from his waistband. Ferris was still on top of him but not for long. Bert rammed an elbow backwards and caught the Major under the ribs, banging all the breath from his stomach. Ferris collapsed in a ball, heaving and choking, his ruddy cheeks growing puce as he made frantic efforts to feed his lungs. Bert scrambled to his feet and aimed his gun downwards.

'You stupid bastard!' he yelled. 'You think we won't kill you? You're a bloody menace!'

'Hold it!' Petrie ran up the aisle, pushing past several passengers who had half risen from their seats to see what was happening. He reached Bert and put a hand on the gun forcing it out of the aim. Petrie looked down at the prone man on the ground. Then at Bert: 'You let a damn fool like that take you!' he said fiercely. 'Stop fooling around with bloody toys and keep your mind on the job. Now get him up!'

Bert bent and hauled Ferris to his feet. The man was still bent double, hands pressed against his bruised ribs and his throat hoarsely seeking air. Bert pushed him backwards until he banged hard against the door of the lavatory.

'You want to go to the lav?' Bert said, opening the door, 'then go. And stay there.'

He pushed Ferris into the lavatory and slammed the door closed.

Petrie gave him another silent warning before returning up the aisle to the pilot's cabin.

'Trouble in the ranks?' Denver asked.

'Nothing we can't handle,' he replied.

'You forgot to tell the passengers the 'plane is wired to explode.'

Petrie moved round to be able to look squarely at the Captain.

'Denver,' he said, half smiling, 'I have every intention of avoiding panic back there. A lot of them are still trying to work out if this is a hi-jack or not. I mean to feed them with just enough information to keep them settled. No rough stuff, keep them informed and they won't be a problem. *You* aren't going to be a problem, are you, Captain?'

'You're the boss.'

'Right. Now shut down and refuel.'

'All right.'

'Get supplies for an eight-hour flight.'

Denver nodded.

'And the tyres,' Petrie said.

'We're going to need a special jack,' Denver said.

'Why?'

'Most airports carry equipment to change one wheel, maybe two at the most. But all of them going at once brings the aircraft down almost on to the ground. You use a special low profile jack to get under and heave it up.'

'You should have thought of that when you removed the anti-skid,' Petrie said.

Denver glanced at him. 'I did,' he replied.

For a long moment the two men stared at each other. Finally: 'Get one,' Petrie said quietly.

'Anything else?'

'Like what?'

'A flight plan to Cuba?'

Petrie smiled. 'All in good time, Captain,' he said and moved back into the passenger area.

Roper blew out his cheeks. 'The cold bloody nerve of the guy,' he said. ' "I have every intention of avoiding panic back there"!'

Denver pressed the sets of switches which closed down the engines.

'That's what I'm worried about,' he said. 'This man sounds as if he's been on a hi-jack course and passed with honours. He's dead right, of course. If they panicked, he wouldn't have a chance. But can you hear anything? Quiet as mice. And about as dangerous. Thank God.'

Petrie walked slowly back up through the subdued passengers. He stopped at the halfway mark in the Economy section.

'Please,' he called, 'no more heroes. We have had one man trying to win a medal. We haven't hurt him but we've put him in a place where he can't endanger the lives of others. I am sorry about the cold. I hope to get the heating on full blast as soon as possible.'

It was true; the people in the front were hugging themselves for warmth. Petrie moved forward and advised the three men in First Class, where the temperature was at freezing point, to move back. The two Danes took up the idea gratefully but the Queen's messenger tugged his topcoat collar round his neck tightly and declined.

The reason for the cold was that the main doors of the Boeing had been opened three feet. A plastic curtain was draped over the gap, an essential accessory on aircraft on the Scandinavian areas in wintertime. If a flight was setting down or picking up, even for twenty minutes, the passengers staying on board would be three parts frostbitten before the escalator had even been wheeled up. The plastic curtain served to prevent the cold air being sucked in or the cabin heat being pulled out.

At present it was stopping the worst of the icy wind from

entering but the seepage was increasing, particularly since Joe was constantly moving past it to look through the gap in the doors. This gave a vision of one hundred and eighty degrees, front, rear and left hand side of the aircraft. Every three minutes he checked the view, especially the acres of airfield behind the tail.

Petrie passed him as he came back through the plastic curtain.

'What's it like?'

Joe blew on his hands.

'Freezing,' he said. 'It's too cold for anyone to try anything. Clear view both ends.'

'Keep checking,' Petrie said. He returned to the cockpit and listened to Denver passing on the requirements to Control.

'Captain,' he said, very quietly. Denver looked up from the microphone after saying: 'Hold it a moment, Control – '

Petrie paused. This time he wasn't smiling.

'I would like you to make it clear to Control that unless this aircraft is fully serviced, repaired, and ready to take off by 5.30 this afternoon, with our friends on board, that's four and a half hours from now, we shall blow it up. There will be no extension to this deadline. Please explain that very carefully.'

Denver watched Petrie after he finished speaking. He knew then and there this man wasn't bluffing.

CHAPTER TEN

Tahlvik pulled his car into a parking area below the Control Tower. He and Barnes stepped out and walked quickly towards the door at the base of the tower.

A police van was disgorging uniformed police, watched by an Inspector. Each man collected a rifle from a stack near the van, signed for it and a box of ammunition and moved on to form a regimented line, waiting for everyone to dismount and arm themselves.

Tahlvik broke his stride and walked over to the Inspector. 'Are you in charge of these men?' he demanded.

The inspector turned and looked him up and down. 'Who the hell are you?' he said.

'It is wise only to swear at people when you know you out-rank them, Inspector,' Tahlvik said mildly. 'My name is Colonel Tahlvik.'

The Inspector succeeded in using deference and hostility at the same time.

'I'm in charge, yes.'

Tahlvik pointed to the line of men standing with their rifles shouldered.

'Get them out of sight and keep them there,' he said.

'I was only following routine procedure,' the Inspector said grudgingly.

'Routine procedure?'

'Yes.'

'Inspector,' Tahlvik said quietly, 'how many hi-jacks have you dealt with?'

'This is the first,' the policeman replied.

'The first. So don't talk to me about routine procedure, mmm?'

The Inspector bit his lip and shot Tahlvik a cold look.

Tahlvik turned to walk back to Barnes, then changed his mind, stopped and came over to the Inspector who was slowly moving towards his men.

'Inspector,' he said. The policeman turned. 'Look,' Tahlvik went on in a low voice empty of command, 'this is my first as well. I'm going to need your help. I'm going to need every bit of help I can get.'

The Inspector smiled bleakly and his hostility melted. 'Very good, sir,' he said.

Tahlvik rejoined Barnes and entered the door of the Control Tower. They caught the lift to the top stage where a flight of steps led up into the centre of operations.

Several technicians stood clustered round the green-tinted windows which allowed a full view of the stranded Boeing two hundred yards away to the right.

As Tahlvik came up the steps into the circular room a middle-aged, worried-looking man detached himself from a group standing round the principal microphone and met him. He held out a hand. 'Matson, head of Airport Authority,' he said crisply.

Tahlvik took the hand without reducing his stride towards the windows. He glared around at the spectators, most of whom were in overalls and played no regular part in the Control Room.

'All right, Matson,' Tahlvik said. 'Let's exert some of that authority. I want this room cleared of everything and everyone but essentials. While you're doing that, I'd like to speak to the pilot.'

Matson led him over to the chief radio controller who sat at a semi-circular desk which slotted into the contours of the room. A small microphone rearing up from a stand was in front of him.

'Contact AC6,' Matson ordered, then went to remove the spectators.

The radio controller spoke into the microphone, calling in the aircraft.

'What's the captain's name?' Tahlvik whispered.

'Denver, sir.'

Denver's voice came over the wire. 'Hello, Control, Denver here.'

Tahlvik motioned to take the chair occupied by the radio controller. He sat down and pulled the microphone towards him.

'Captain Denver,' he said, 'my name is Colonel Tahlvik, I am a member of the Nordlandic armed forces with special duties connected with national security.'

'Pleased to meet you, Colonel,' Denver replied. 'A pity about the circumstances, though.'

Tahlvik paused. Would Denver know the general code words agreed upon by the various airline pilots' associations?

'How are you, Captain?' Tahlvik said, making each word stand up on end.

Another pause.

'Lonely, Colonel,' came the reply, 'but not for long.'

Tahlvik dropped the stilted delivery and spoke rapidly.

'How are the passengers?'

'They're quiet, but they haven't been told about the explosives.'

'Do you believe the 'plane is wired up?'

'Colonel, we have a cool pro on board here,' Denver said with chilling conviction. 'He's well trained and they've all got guns. I'm lucky to have got away with what I did on landing, except I know he needs me to take off again. I blew out all the tyres by removing the anti-skid and jamming on the brakes. That isn't as suicidal as it sounds. Once I'd touched down and reduced speed a 'plane will stand it. Anyway, I reckoned we could all do with a delayed take-off.'

'Thanks, Captain,' Tahlvik said. 'We can.'

He waited five seconds before the silence was broken again. This time the voice belonged to someone else.

'Colonel Tahlvik?' it said.

'Who is this?'

52

'I asked for refuelling. Where is it ?'

As he listened Tahlvik reached inside a pocket and withdrew a miniature tape recorder. He placed it silently down next to the microphone and switched it on.

'You are called Petrie ?' he said, spinning out the words until the recorder was in place and running.

'Screw who I am. Where are the ground crew services ?'

'They're in hand – '

'Colonel,' Petrie said, cutting in, 'let's start by cutting out the bullshit. We need fuel for an eight-hour flight and we need it now. So get the lead out and have the cart sent over right away. Two, we need drinking water, sterilised milk for two babies on board and a first aid kit would be handy. No one's been hurt yet and I'd like to think it'll stay that way, but you never know when some Tarzan type might try and get smart.

'Tranquillisers will help as well for some of the more nervous ones. Three, since Captain Denver deliberately burst all our tyres when he landed we need a special low-profile jack. Now hear this well, Tahlvik. You have until 5.30 to release the people in the embassy, bring them here and put them on board. You have until 5.30 to repair this aircraft, refuel it and have it prepared for take-off. There will be no extension to this deadline, as I've already explained to the captain. If one of these demands, just one, isn't met by that time, I shall blow us all up.'

Everyone in the Control Room heard Petrie lay out his list of requirements in dead silence. When he finished, they looked at Tahlvik.

Tahlvik sat and stared at the microphone. Then he looked up at the circle of expectant faces. He stood and glanced at his watch.

'I'm going to lunch,' he said.

He nodded to Barnes and Matson to follow him, crossed to the stairs and went down to the lift.

'Shall I close down the airport ?' Matson asked as they went.

'No,' Tahlvik said. 'Keep it open. I'm not going to let them paralyse the whole country.'

They squeezed into the tiny lift.

'Denver was right,' Tahlvik remarked. 'He's a professional.'

'Yes,' Matson said and let out a long sigh. 'Why couldn't we have had a nice simple basket case?'

'What about this jack?'

'We don't have one.'

'Why not?'

'There's never any call,' Matson said. 'They're kept mainly at the manufacturing works.'

'There's a call now,' Tahlvik reminded him as they stepped out of the lift at the bottom and moved to the exit doors of the Control Tower.

'Try the military, try anywhere near by, but get it.'

'It will take time,' Matson remarked.

Tahlvik turned and looked quickly at him as they pushed through the doors and moved into the freezing cold outside.

'Take all the time you want, Matson,' he said. 'As long as it's here inside two hours.'

The older man smiled and moved off in a different direction towards a block of offices adjacent to the terminal buildings. Tahlvik and Barnes continued until they entered a building which numbered among the signs running down the side of the entrance: 'Canteen – Staff Only'.

Tahlvik stopped at the entrance. 'Frank,' he said, 'get on to your people, Scotland Yard, Special Branch. Find out if there is anything known on a Ray Petrie. If possible, I'd like to know a bit more about who we're dealing with.'

Barnes nodded and followed Matson.

'Oh, and Frank,' Tahlvik called. The Englishman stopped and turned round. 'We're going to need an office. Ask Matson what he can do. Somewhere in the Control Tower, if possible. A room that overlooks the 'plane.'

'I'll try,' Barnes called and hurried after Matson.

Tahlvik followed the signs to the canteen. A public telephone booth stood outside the canteen doors. Tahlvik fumbled for a coin, slotted it into the machine and dialled a number.

'Colonel Donner, please,' he said. 'Colonel Tahlvik speaking. Tell him, please, that this is most urgent.'

He waited for almost a minute before Donner came to the telephone. 'Well, now, Nils,' he said. 'Don't tell me where you are calling from.'

'You know where I am,' Tahlvik said. 'I want you here. And bring half a dozen of your best commandos.'

'I heard the order was to give in,' Donner said.

'That's right,' Tahlvik replied tersely. 'Can you get here in thirty minutes?'

He replaced the telephone and walked into the busy, bustling canteen. It was in the middle of the lunch period and a long queue stretched back from the cafeteria counters.

A television screen stared down from a far wall facing the members of the queue as they picked out their food and shuffled towards the pay desk. The still image showing on the screen was that of the Boeing lying at an angle in the unkempt fields of the airport. The photograph had been taken with a long-range telephoto lens and the outline was blurred. A voice spoke over the still, a newscaster filling in time with a padded version of what had happened so far.

'We are unable to show the actual scene live,' he was saying, 'due to a clamp down on all newspaper and television cameras while the present very difficult situation is going on.'

Tahlvik picked a tray from a pile at the end of the line and waited patiently to move up to the food compartments.

A few minutes after he joined the crew he saw a photograph of himself appear on the screen ahead. 'Colonel Tahlvik is in charge of operations at the airport,' the commentator was saying. 'He is a professional soldier who has spent most of his career trying to prevent wars rather than fight them. He has served in several peacekeeping forces throughout the world including the difficult areas of Korea in 1953 and the Congo in 1960. But here today he faces a grave situation. The lives of one

55

hundred people hang in the balance as Tahlvik wrestles with the dilemma. The country holds its breath waiting to discover if common sense will prevail. How, one wonders, is Colonel Tahlvik viewing *this* campaign ?'

A number of people passing by craned their necks in surprise as their eyes moved from the image on the television screen to Tahlvik standing in line before the cafeteria shelves. He ignored them. He felt the usual twinge of irritation as he heard the army treated by some pimply youth with the kind of trendy contempt so much in vogue during the last few years. Pimply youths themselves were of no consequence. Only when they had access to the ubiquitous television sets did they take on another dimension. 'How is Tahlvik viewing *this* campaign – ' The same innuendo that Bernhard had made. 'There's no acceptable level of casualties here, you know.' He imagined viewers all over the country listening to this commentator and saying to themselves 'Leave the army in charge and those passengers don't stand a chance.'

He would never come out of this day's work successfully. He wouldn't accept himself if he caved in. The public wouldn't accept him unless he managed to free the passengers. If the issue were to be decided on democratic lines, he should turn about, march back to the Control Tower and order the instant release of Shepherd and his people, place them on board the Boeing and wave them off. But as in war, solutions are not arrived at democratically. The strong, the most cunning, the sly survive; the others go to the wall. The question that returned to nag his brain ceaselessly was: which of the two was he ? Was he strong or weak ?

He paid for his food and weaved in and out of the tables, trying to find one completely empty. Four people stood to leave in the corner and Tahlvik took their place. He was laying out his plates and cutlery when Barnes came to the door and looked round the room. He saw Tahlvik and came over, accompanied by a good-looking, well-dressed woman in her late forties.

56

Tahlvik didn't see them until they had arrived at the table and looked up in surprise when Barnes spoke. 'Colonel,' he said, then turned and looked at the woman, 'this is Mrs Palmer.'

Tahlvik stood up and shook hands with her. She looked tired. Her face was pinched and drawn and her hair knotted where nervous fingers had intertwined the locks above her forehead. Tahlvik pulled out a chair and she sat down. Barnes remained on his feet.

'I was out of the house when it happened – ' she started to say.

'At church,' Tahlvik said.

'Yes, of course,' she said, angry at herself, and confused. 'You must know all about it.'

'Your husband explained this morning,' he said. 'He is well.'

Mrs Palmer looked across at him with tired eyes. Until Barnes had brought her across he had felt hungry. Now his stomach was contracting and the food in front of him no longer had any appeal. He had always been able to sense an unpleasant scene. This one wasn't going to be nasty. Just unappetising.

'He is *not* well, Colonel,' she replied.

'He has been receiving his medicine throughout,' he said.

'My husband,' Mrs Palmer replied very quietly, 'is dying.'

Tahlvik placed down his knife and fork. He was thirsty but he knew he was unable to pick up the ice-cold tumbler of milk now, not while she was at the table.

'It's his heart,' she continued. 'The pills do nothing but give him some borrowed time. I should say they do a lot for him, except they won't provide a cure. He knows about it. He knows he has a year at the most *if* – she paused a second, ' – he avoids any kind of strain.'

The implication was clear and Tahlvik absorbed it without an outward reaction.

'We're doing all we can, Mrs Palmer,' he said.

'No, you are not,' she answered. She spoke in a quiet, level way which only increased the effect of her words. 'He has already been held for two whole days. Now, here, it looks like there will be more delays, more waiting. More strain on him which he can't endure. Colonel,' Mrs Palmer continued, her voice softening, 'I've spent thirty years as the wife of a diplomat. In all that time I have never broken the cardinal rule of the diplomatic game. I have never interfered in the politics of another country. Well, now I am. I am begging you to let these men go. These men holding my husband are killing him as surely as if they were tightening a rope around his neck. Let them go, please, Colonel. They'll be caught somewhere else. Somehow. But I implore you, let them go from here.'

Tahlvik said nothing. He glanced up at Barnes and made it clear with one look that he didn't relish the idea of sharing a lunch table with someone who was crucifying his conscience.

Barnes took the hint and bent, placed a hand gently on her arm. Mrs Palmer stood, never taking her eyes off Tahlvik and let Barnes lead her away and out of the canteen. They passed Matson who stopped and spoke to them. Barnes pointed towards Tahlvik and Matson came over.

'Petrie has asked for a police two-way radio for himself and for Shepherd in the Ambassador's house,' he said.

Tahlvik thought a moment, then nodded. 'Give Shepherd his,' he said, 'but keep Petrie's back until I say so. And get me one too.'

'Very well. Oh, and Colonel, you have an office. It's just below the Control Room in the Tower. There is intercommunication between the two.'

'Thank you.'

Matson walked off. Tahlvik tried to apply himself to the food again but his appetite had gone. He pushed the plates away, gulped down the milk and stood up to leave.

The television screen was showing a series of *vox pop* interviews with men in the street. They were being asked how they felt about the hi-jackers and their demands.

'Well, it's nothing to do with us, is it,' one man said, looking apprehensively down at the microphone almost stuffed up one of his nostrils. 'I mean, the only thing that matters are those poor people on board. We ought to get them off as soon as possible and give the men holding them anything they want . . .'

Tahlvik left the canteen as another man standing in a snow-covered street was saying:

'There's no *problem* here, I'm surprised you used that word. We simply get rid of these foreign gangsters and at the same time protect our own nationals aboard the airplane and all the other innocent bystanders . . .'

Outside Barnes was waiting for him and they strolled back towards the Tower.

'I'm sorry about – well, I hardly had much choice with Mrs Palmer,' Barnes said.

'That's all right,' Tahlvik shrugged. They were walking past the parking lot under the Control Tower. One of the cars, a large black Austin Princess bore a small Union Jack on the radiator. A driver was dozing behind the wheel.

'Denver says they are all stiff with guns,' Tahlvik said. 'What the hell is London airport playing at ? Find out if they're using their magnetometers, the amount of security they're carrying out.'

'O.K.'

'Unless you can come up with some idea how four men carry an arsenal on board plus, remember, enough explosive to destroy the entire 'plane.'

Barnes shrugged. 'I haven't the faintest,' he said.

'There's always a chance,' Tahlvik went on, 'they are kidding about blowing it up. But it's a chance I'm not going to rely on. Denver thinks Petrie's a pro and so do I. A pro wouldn't set down here without some kind of teeth in his final ultimatum.'

Tahlvik continued to talk on as they moved towards the base of the Control Tower, although he was thinking aloud rather than holding a conversation with Barnes. 'He says he intends to blow them all up at 5.30. I have to believe he will.'

Barnes sneaked a look at his watch. Tahlvik saw him.

'1.15,' he said. 'Four hours left. And we haven't even started to get the most preliminary questions answered.'

A fuel cart was being assembled at the edge of the tarmac in front of the Tower. Matson was talking to one of the men. He saw Tahlvik and hurried over.

'Petrie's beginning to scream for his refuelling,' Matson said.

'Let him,' Tahlvik replied. 'He's given us five hours. He's not going anywhere for a while. What about the jack?'

'I have a man calling every possible source.'

'And the radios?'

'They are in the stores here. Ten minutes.'

Tahlvik nodded. He turned to watch an armoured truck which was slowly advancing up the long road leading to the main entrance of the airport. Barnes was looking in the same direction, frowning. 'London Airport, Frank,' he said. Barnes grinned, suppressing his curiosity about the approaching truck, and entered the Tower.

The armoured car ground to a halt behind the Tower. There were two men in the front. One was a uniformed colonel in his early fifties. Donner. A stocky, tough frame, without a spare inch of flesh. He saw Tahlvik, jumped down and walked over, using a sailor's rolling gait.

'Still having problems?' Donner said, a broad grin spreading over his face.

'Just a few,' Tahlvik replied. They were old friends and Tahlvik was glad to see him. 'You didn't waste any time.'

'I brought eight men,' he said, pointing at the armoured vehicle. 'All of them are good.'

Tahlvik led the way to the Tower. 'They will need to be,' he said.

They took the lift to the floor below the Control Tower. One of the Control Tower staff was waiting on the landing.

'Colonel Tahlvik?' he asked. Tahlvik said yes and the official opened a door with a set of keys.

'Lars Matson said you wanted an office,' he said, going in. 'This do?'

Tahlvik crossed to the windows and looked out. The Boeing was well in sight to the right.

The official pressed an intercommunication box, flicking a switch up and down. A voice said:

'Control Room.'

The official said 'just testing, Control Room,' and flicked the switch up again.

'This is fine,' Tahlvik said. 'Thank you.'

The official left, closing the door.

The two soldiers gazed out over the frozen airfield towards the hi-jacked 737.

'What chance has anyone got of reaching that plane undetected?' Tahlvik asked.

Donner pulled out a pair of binoculars strung round his neck and nestling inside his greatcoat. He scanned the flat wastelands behind the aircraft. To one side, about two hundred yards from the 'plane, ran the airfield perimeter road. Between the road and the edge of the tarmac was a large hangar.

Donner brought down the binoculars. 'About a thousand to one,' he said.

'What odds do your men accept?' Tahlvik asked.

'Two thousand to one,' Donner grinned.

'You brought eight?'

'Yes. I can call for more. They're standing by – '

'No,' Tahlvik said. 'Not yet. Eight men. All right. Go downstairs and select the best one. Then work out a way he can reach the 'plane and climb in through the hatch door situated immediately below the pilot's cabin. Having done that, tell him how to overpower four heavily armed hi-jackers while at the same time not harming the hair on the head of one passenger. He will have one chance. If he fails, they will most likely kill him. He will, of course have the choice of turning the mission down. He probably will if he has any imagination. But I tell you, Donner,' Tahlvik said, and for the first time he sounded bleak, 'it's about the only chance we have.'

CHAPTER ELEVEN

Palmer felt a sudden spasm of pain across his chest and closed his eyes in an effort to stay silent until it passed. His last pill had been taken only two hours ago. Another two before the next was due. He moved in the chair, trying to sit upright. a cold dampness started up above his temples. Sweat.

Eva sat behind him and turned as he moved.

'All right?' she asked. He nodded.

'In the circumstances,' he replied.

'Shouldn't be long now,' Eva said, including the housekeepers in her address.

'It wouldn't be very convenient for you if I should die, now would it,' Palmer said. He smiled at the thought. 'Really bad luck for you.'

Shepherd, his mask in place, came under the curtain.

'We still have them,' he said, pointing to the elderly couple.

'Yes,' Palmer said. He knew Shepherd relied upon him, the Ambassador, to work the blackmail, not a couple of harmless old people but he was not about to say it and scare them to death. But he could see Shepherd had taken his point. He smiled again.

'Are you trying to be a hero, Palmer?' Shepherd asked. 'Or are you just a fool?'

'I have sat here for two days,' Palmer replied, 'trying to determine the very same question about you.'

'Have you decided?'

'Not completely.'

'I can hardly imagine your kind calling us heroes,' Shepherd said. 'So we are therefore fools.'

'Not necessarily,' Palmer replied. After a while, he added: 'You are, I take it, the people who have caused so much trouble in Britain during the past few years.'

Shepherd didn't reply.

'The sabotage,' Palmer went on, 'and the killing.'

Shepherd reacted at the second half of Palmer's comment. The mask flicked back to face the Ambassador.

'Of which you disapprove?' Shepherd asked curtly.

'I should have thought that was self-evident,' Palmer answered.

Shepherd leaned against the table, looking down at the bound captive.

'Your disapproval wasn't self evident in 1941,' he said quietly, a gently mocking tone in his voice.

Palmer reacted slightly. He glanced upwards and met the two holes in the mask. A pair of eyes glittered behind them.

'You served four years in Yugoslavia,' Shepherd went on. 'With Tito's partisans. From what I read everyone in the Yugoslav Resistance spent the war butchering Germans, blowing up power stations and railway lines. Even when the Germans started to take reprisals, wipe out entire villages in retaliation, they carried on. I can't believe you were there just as an observer. A non-combatant. Were you, Mr Palmer?'

'That was war –' Palmer began but knew the argument about to hit him before he started.

'So is this,' Shepherd said quickly. 'Why did you fight Germany? I'll tell you – God knows your generation never get tired of saying why: you fought to destroy a system you considered evil. Right?'

Palmer said nothing.

'Right,' Shepherd continued. 'Well, so am I. So are we. We have declared a state of war to exist between ourselves and the Government and we shan't stop fighting until we are either dead – or it's destroyed.'

'Britain declared war in '39,' Palmer said, 'because Germany had torn up treaties entered into in good faith with allies we had sworn to help defend. We replied to an act of aggression with the only weapon we had – war.'

'That's correct,' Shepherd said. He was warming to the

subject and his delivery became even more like an eloquent legal appeal. 'The British Government has torn up treaties it made to the people. Election promises, pledges to remove cancers in our society. It helps to keep foreign tyrannies in power while publicly denouncing them. It has done all that we accused the Germans of on both the occasions we went to war with them. The people are fully justified in declaring war on those who run their country. Which is precisely what we have done.'

Mike called from the hallway. 'Policeman approaching.'

Shepherd bent down and stooped under the curtain. He moved to the window and looked out down the path.

A solitary policeman was walking towards the house. Over a shoulder he carried a canvas bag with a large strap.

'What is that?' Shepherd asked.

'A radio,' Mike replied.

'Petrie must have sent it,' Shepherd said. 'Bring it in.'

Mike ran through the hall to the door. The policeman dropped the set on to the step and walked away. Mike reached out and pulled it inside. He unclipped the canvas bag and examined the machine. Shepherd came through.

'Well?'

'I've used one like this before,' Mike said. He yanked out the collapsible aerial full stretch and began to turn the tuning dial slowly round, holding the set an inch from his ear. Several voices came and went amid the crackling. Shepherd watched Mike as he completed the cycle of the wavebands.

'No one there,' he said.

'Keep trying,' Shepherd replied. 'There will be.'

CHAPTER TWELVE

Tahlvik stood by the window in his office beneath the Tower and kept his binoculars trained on the distant perimeter road beyond the Boeing. Donner had sent his man in a jeep bumping round the edge of the airfield, keeping out of sight of the hijacked aircraft and Tahlvik estimated he ought to be arriving at the hangar two hundred yards directly behind the tail.

Below him a technician waited in an airport truck with a radio set on the seat next to him. He was looking up at Tahlvik's window.

Tahlvik looked at his watch, then down at the man below him. He nodded, then made a movement with the palms of his hands, pressing them downwards telling the man to take it slowly.

The intercom on his desk sprang into life.

'Hey, Tahlvik, where's my radio?' Petrie's voice.

'Coming out now,' Tahlvik replied. He looked beyond the truck now on a snow path out to the 'plane. The fuel carts were also rumbling on to the tarmac heading the same way.

'And your refuelling,' Tahlvik added into the box.

Next to the intercom lay Tahlvik's own pocket-sized recorder, the tape slowly turning.

'About time,' Petrie said. Then the box went dead.

Beyond the Boeing, Donner's commando was dismounting the jeep and running quickly along a path cleared through the snow to the wall of the hangar. He was dressed in white sweater, white trousers and plimsolls and easily merged with the landscape.

He approached the edge of the hangar and looked round, out towards the target. He checked his Smith & Wesson .38 and stuck it back in his belt under the sweater.

Then he set off, coming out into the open, jog-trotting

towards the tail of the aircraft. He kept to a direct route leading up to the tail but stayed slightly to the right. The blind side out of sight of the man who stood by the open doors. Donner had drawn the route carefully on a diagram. They had seen only one look-out; no one was checking the other side of the 'plane. To do that someone would have to be stationed in the open in order to spot an approach from the rear.

Tahlvik watched the figure cross the two hundred yards, occasionally losing him against the white backdrop of snow.

The commando was halfway across when there was a flurry of activity at the door of Tahlvik's office. He heard a woman's voice say: 'Let me go, I must see him!'

He turned to see Mrs Palmer push past Barnes and enter the room. She stumbled to the window and pointed towards the commando, turning furiously on Tahlvik. 'What are you doing?'

Tahlvik turned angrily on Barnes. 'Get her out of here!'

She banged the window with her fist.

'You can't, you can't try and stop them!' she shouted. 'They'll kill my husband, they'll kill everyone! Can't you see that? Don't you believe they'll do it!'

Barnes took hold of her arm and resisted her attempts to shake him off.

'Come on, Mrs Palmer, please,' he pleaded, 'Come away. Colonel Tahlvik knows what he's doing – '

'So do I!' she cried. 'He's risking my husband's life to prove how clever he is, that's what he's doing!'

Barnes was pulling her towards the door. She turned: 'Why aren't you out there?' she said. 'You send others to do the dangerous work while you sit here!'

Then she was out the door. Tahlvik strode across the room and yelled after Barnes: 'Put a guard on this door. No one comes in here unless *I* say so!'

He brought up a leg and slammed the door shut with a kick.

When he returned to the window the commando was almost up to the tail. He watched the figure duck and disappear underneath.

Turning to the intercom he pressed a switch.

'Hello, AC six,' he said.

Denver's voice came on. 'Yes, Colonel.'

'Captain, how are you?'

'Lonely.'

Tahlvik dropped his voice and spoke quickly.

'Denver, one of my men is under your forward hold. He's armed. Bring him in when you can. All right?'

A pause before: 'Thank you, Control. I confirm heating is now back to normal.'

Tahlvik heard Petrie's voice in the background say: 'Yes, things are hotting up nicely,' before he switched the connection off.

Underneath the belly of the 737 the commando crouched as he crept towards the front half of the fuselage. The hatch was exactly where Donner had said. Quickly he took the metal strip from his pocket and started untwisting the clips holding it in place. It took him thirty seconds before he took the weight of the hatch and slowly lowered it. It stayed swinging heavily on a pair of hinges, a foot from the ground. The commando reached up inside the hold and groped for something to grasp. Then he pulled his body upwards inside.

The hold was dark and cramped and the commando had to wriggle upwards painfully before his body rested entirely inside. He put a hand above his head and felt the metal plate separating him from the space immediately behind the pilot's cabin.

Above him Denver sat in his seat as Petrie stood behind looking through the windscreen. He flicked his finger and Denver passed him the microphone.

'Tahlvik – '

'What do you want, Petrie?'

'Our people. Where are they?'

'Their release is being discussed. It takes time.'

'It's better not take too much time.'

Petrie glanced at a watch attached on his wrist above the detonator system.

'I have 1.45. Don't forget what I said. No extension to the deadline.'

'I'm hardly likely to,' Tahlvik replied.

Petrie handed back the microphone and left the cabin. Denver waited, then eased himself from his seat.

'Where are you going?' Roper asked.

He watched Denver put a finger to his lips, then kneel down at the entrance to the cabin. He pulled back the carpeting and knocked three times with his knuckles on the steel plate below. Roper looked puzzled, then even more so when the knocks were answered below.

Denver started quickly to unlock the clips holding down the hatch. He had two off when he was aware that the cabin door had opened again.

He looked up. He stared straight into the barrel of Petrie's gun. Petrie was smiling.

In the hold below, the commando waited for the hatch cover to be lifted off. He had exchanged the knocks. Everything ought to be clear above. He rested a hand on the bulk under his sweater that was his gun. He ran the other hand round the cover, trying to gauge the width. He couldn't afford to be trapped halfway through. It meant a clean passage up and over, and somewhere along the line he had to draw the gun –

He heard a quiet cough beneath him. He looked down past his legs and feet which stood astride the hatch.

A man was crouched under the hole. He held a gun which was pointing directly up into the hold. The commando froze with fear, then impulsively reached for his own weapon.

'Don't!' the man below him barked.

The commando obeyed when he saw he would not even grasp the butt of his revolver before the other would put a bullet into his stomach.

'Come down,' the man underneath ordered as he moved a yard to one side.

The commando bent, lowered himself through the hatch hole and dropped to the tarmac. He turned to face the man with the gun. A shiver passed through his body as he prepared himself for death. He wanted to plead to be spared but training and other undefined reasons prevented him. The other man leaned over and extracted the gun from his waistband and stuck it in his own.

'On your way,' he said. 'Keep your hands on your head.'

For a moment the commando stayed transfixed to the spot. 'You're a lucky man, matey.'

The commando turned and walked away, his hands linked by the fingers behind his head. He wanted to run but kept a regular stride back towards the Control Tower.

The man, Bert, watched him until he was a hundred yards away and then sprinted round to the entrance of the aircraft where a small escalator reached down from the door. In a few moments he had run up the ladder which Joe pulled in after him.

Tahlvik stood next to his window watching. His fists clenched at his sides.

The intercom buzzed. He leaned over and switched it on.

'I promise you, Tahlvik,' he heard Petrie say, 'the next one you send will die.'

Tahlvik stayed by the window, hardly listening. Then another voice came over the intercom. It was Barnes. 'This is Captain Barnes of the British Embassy,' he said.

Tahlvik guessed he must be speaking into the radio controller's mike upstairs with which he was connected.

'We are negotiating the release of your men with the authorities. But I warn you, they will refuse outright if there is any loss of life. Is – that – clear?'

The last sentence was heavily emphasised. Petrie didn't answer at once.

'It's clear to me,' he said. 'But is it clear to Colonel Tahlvik? You tell him what you've just told me.'

Tahlvik left his office. A civilian guard stood outside the door and closed it for him as he sprinted upstairs.

Donner was in the Control Room looking despondently out through the green windows, watching his man approach the Tower.

Tahlvik hurried into the room and made for Donner. Barnes was standing next to the radio controller's microphone. Matson was on the telephone. He saw Tahlvik and cupped a hand over the receiver.

'They've located a jack, Colonel,' he called.

Tahlvik didn't acknowledge him as he went up to Donner. He pointed angrily at the commando below them.

'Your best man!' he said bitterly. 'They saw him all the way.'

'Impossible,' Donner replied quietly.

Tahlvik dropped his voice. 'Then what went wrong? You tell me.'

Donner was calm but firm. 'He kept to the blind side. They couldn't have seen him.'

'Well, someone did,' Tahlvik said, still angry.

'Yes,' Donner answered. He brought up his binoculars and began to pan slowly over the airfield boundaries.

Tahlvik watched him. Donner moved his head slowly round in an arc. Then he stopped and retraced the binoculars an inch.

'Someone saw him,' Donner said, 'but not from *inside* the 'plane.'

He handed the binoculars to Tahlvik, pointing. 'There's some kind of observation post just above the perimeter fence,' he said. 'Looks like a bunker left over from the war.'

Tahlvik looked through the binoculars. He brought a grey concrete hump into focus. In the front, facing the airfield, was a slit like a large letterbox. As he watched he saw a glint of metal framed by the darkness of the slit.

'There's someone up there,' Tahlvik said, handing the glasses back.

Donner had another look.

'That's how it was done,' he said. 'No wonder he didn't stand a chance.'

'At least they didn't kill him,' Tahlvik muttered.

Donner went to leave the room.

'Who are you sending over there?' Tahlvik called after him.

'I'll take four men,' Donner replied.

'Can you make that five?' Tahlvik asked. Something put Mrs Palmer's words into his mind.

'If you like,' Donner said and Tahlvik followed him out.

As they drove away from the Control Tower, five of them in an airport truck, the fuel cart was hooking its hoses up to the 737. The technician had delivered the radio and was driving back again.

Donner drove, with Tahlvik next to him in front. They dipped down and followed the perimeter road behind the various hangars and outlying buildings where ancient, gutted frames of aeroplanes lay strewn around. Some of them could have been there since World War Two. Some of them certainly dated from the '40s. They looked sad and forgotten as they stood blackened and silent under a crown of snow.

They bumped along the road beyond the perimeter fence which ran along the top of a bank ten yards above them. When they neared the area of the bunker Donner slowed.

'What purpose does the bunker serve?' Tahlvik asked. Donner shrugged.

'I remember coming here not long after the war,' he said. 'They were built then. They're still kept up, I suppose, by the civil defence.'

'What for?'

'Who knows?'

Donner grinned and stopped the truck. He motioned everyone to dismount. He brought out a map of the airport, opened it up over the bonnet. He stabbed a point on the perimeter.

'We are here,' he said. 'Our objective is, or should be, here – '

He moved his finger an inch. 'Round the next bend.'

He folded the map and stuffed it away and led the other four along the snow-covered bank until they came to the bend.

Donner looked round. A large entrance, which looked as if it had been crudely boarded up at some time, lay set into the bank. As he crept nearer they saw it was an entrance to the base of a huge solid beehive construction made of reinforced concrete.

Donner nodded to his men who split up without a word, two crossing the road and looking at the entrance head-on, from behind an old hut. They drew their guns and held them steady, pointing at the entrance while the others reached it under their cover.

Everyone remained silent. Donner signalled the men providing cover to stay where they were. Then he and Tahlvik cautiously climbed over the frozen snow to the entrance.

About a dozen long planks had been nailed over the concrete entrance which stood about six feet high. Tahlvik touched the two middle planks. They came away easily.

Peering through into the gloom Tahlvik could make out, on either side of the entrance, several stacks of military crates. They left a narrow corridor in the centre which led to another entrance leading into the heart of the bunker. Donner signalled for one man to accompany himself and Tahlvik, the other to wait by the main entrance.

He and Tahlvik were first through the gap in the planks and lowered themselves gently to the floor. It wasn't gentle enough; all four feet created a loud crunching noise as they landed which froze them in their tracks. Looking down, they saw the concrete floor was covered in broken glass. It lay like a gleaming carpet stretching up into the darkness of the gangway between the boxes. Tahlvik bent and picked up a piece of a beer bottle. He held it up to Donner: 'Someone celebrated the end of the war in here,' he muttered.

Moving cautiously they crept between the stacks of crates towards the next door. Glass tinkled beneath them as they slid their feet along the ground, pushing the splinters away rather than crushing them under foot. At the door they paused.

Visibility was now down to two or three feet and they knew even this distance would shorten once they lost sight of the main entrance. Ahead of them lay a steep incline leading up to the observation post. Donner drew a revolver and put himself in front of Tahlvik. The third man brought up the rear.

Step by cautious step they advanced into the pitch black of the corridor. Tahlvik felt above him. His hand came in contact with a rough-hewn ceiling which allowed a height in the corridor of about five feet. Fortunately the beer party of long ago had not ventured this far and their feet met a cushion of damp slime over the floor which went some way to deaden their footfalls.

They climbed for about ten yards before the blackness was pierced by a sliver of daylight. Tahlvik ran into Donner's back as he stopped. They waited, then moved on more slowly.

The daylight increased but very slowly. They were still a long way from the observation slit which had to be the source. Suddenly their footsteps sounded very loud and as if by telepathy all three began to place their boots down more carefully. Tahlvik wished he had brought a gun.

In the glimmering light the corridor levelled out and in front of them, five yards away was a broken-down door. Light streamed through the vertical planks which had been nailed together across a Z-shaped frame. The door had been closed across the corridor but it dangled from one hinge; its usefulness had long since departed.

Donner moved forwards in slow motion, tiptoeing to the doorway. Tahlvik came behind him trying to keep to the places where he placed his feet. They heard a scuffle from the other side of the ruined door and stopped. Then a quiet cough sounded.

Through the gaps in the door they saw a bunker room about twenty feet across and ten wide. A man stood with his back to them looking through the observation slit. Both arms were up in front of him and he seemed to be staring out through binoculars. At his side in the gloom below the peephole was a long metal structure leaning against the wall. Other equipment lay near his feet, unidentifiable in the half light.

Donner looked at Tahlvik and inclined his head towards the room, indicating a rush inside. Tahlvik nodded; so did the commando. Donner brought his revolver up so that the barrel pointed upwards, hugging it to his chest. He leaned a shoulder on the broken down door and giving a quick nod to the others, leaned hard on it. The door crashed flat as the remaining hinge came away on the jamb and the three men hurled themselves inside. The man at the aperture only had time to turn, look astonished before he was hit by a combined force of about four hundred and fifty pounds. The air raced from his mouth as from a burst tyre but he was prevented from crumpling by Tahlvik and Donner who grabbed an arm each and pinned him back against the wall. The commando ran his hands over the gasping man's body, up round his shoulder blades then down his sides. He looked at Donner and shook his head. Donner pulled on the arm he held and the man spun round to face the wall.

'All right,' he said, 'who are you and what are you doing here?'

Even had the man wanted to talk he lacked the air in his lungs to do so. Flattened face first against the wall his throat rasped as he tried to catch his breath and Donner had to support most of his weight.

The commando took the man's wallet from his inside pocket and opened it up. Tahlvik meanwhile was looking more closely at the equipment on the floor. What had looked like a rifle propped against the wall was, in fact, a camera tripod. The other pieces lying around were all parts of a photographer's paraphernalia: two cameras, numerous telephoto lenses, range-finders.

Tahlvik only had time to glance up at Donner before the commando stepped forward.

'Sir' – he said. Tahlvik took a small square card the man held, taken from the wallet. It read: 'PARIS MATCH'. On the obverse side was one word printed large: 'PRESSE'.

Tahlvik showed it to Donner who let go of the man. No one spoke for some time, the soldiers because they were at a loss for words, the photographer because he was at a loss for breath.

The photographer recovered first. A hoarse stream of French invective started, gathering speed as he straightened up, massaging his stomach.

Tahlvik was looking through the observation hole.

'He has to be out there somewhere,' he said. 'And we can do nothing until we find him.'

CHAPTER THIRTEEN

Mike looked up from the radio set. 'I've got them,' he said.

Shepherd came across and listened. A voice, rising and falling with the atmospherics was saying 'Hello, Sunflower, come in Sunflower, this is Petrie, come in Sunflower – '

'Hello, Petrie,' Mike said, his lips brushing the speaker, 'this is Sunflower, We read you. This is Sunflower – '

He handed the set to Shepherd who was holding out his hand. 'Sunflower speaking,' he said. 'Ray?'

There was a pause at the other end and a different voice came on. 'Hi, Sunflower. You got your set O.K.'

'Yes, thank you. What is happening at your end?'

'We have a repair job,' Petrie said. 'Shouldn't take too long. They've found a jack and said it should be here within the hour.'

Shepherd gripped the set tightly. 'Listen, Ray,' he said, and a trace of nervousness tinged his voice. He wasn't used to asking for favours and the task didn't come easily to him. 'We have our hostages, we have transport. Why can't we come out to you now?'

'Don't do that, Sunflower,' Petrie said after a second's hesitation. 'We are stronger apart at the moment.'

'In what way?' Shepherd said. He mustn't show that the siege in the house was beginning to erode his self control. 'How are we stronger?'

'You have hostages,' Petrie's voice said, dimming a little as the waveband faltered, 'so have we. I'm your insurance, you are mine, you dig?'

'Yes, but – ' He stopped, cleared his throat. 'Very well, Ray, you are in charge. But keep this line open. I would like to remain in contact.'

'Check. Patience, brother. All is cool. We'll be away in just a few hours now. Out.'

Shepherd handed the set slowly back to Mike who gave him a nervous glance.

'Nothing wrong, is there?' he asked.

Shepherd shook his head. 'He knows what he's doing,' he repeated. 'I would play it the same way. As long as the 'plane can't take off, it's better that we are here than on board. He's right.'

Mike returned to his lookout point in the house, taking the set with him. Shepherd wandered towards the fireplace. The ashes were dead now and the room was chilled. He stared down at the embers, holding on to the mantelpiece. Then he turned, rapping his shin against a coffee table behind him. He bit his lip, looked down at the table, then brought back a foot and kicked the table flying across the room. It struck the wall with a crash, gouged a hole in the plaster and fell to the carpet.

CHAPTER FOURTEEN

'I'm sorry, sir, but a search of the entire airport, all the buildings, will take at least five hours.'

The Police Inspector stood by the door of Tahlvik's office facing Tahlvik who stared out of the window. There was more regret in his voice than irritation that he should be asked to do the impossible. After the business earlier with his men and their rifles he had quickly come to respect this direct, blunt soldier who now appeared to be facing helpless defeat. He wanted to help. He could say they might be able to do it in four hours, but he knew that wasn't much help. It was now 2.15 and in just over three hours the hi-jackers had promised to detonate the explosives inside the aircraft.

'I know,' Tahlvik said. He turned and gave the man a bleak smile. 'You are right, of course. How many men do you have downstairs?'

'Twenty-two, Colonel.'

Tahlvik turned back to the window.

'Take those perimeter buildings first,' he said pointing off to the left. 'Start at the top and work downwards. Anyone on the roof could overlook the whole field. They could certainly have given them the tip-off about the man we sent out.' He grinned. 'Better than standing around getting frostbite.'

The Inspector smiled and saluted. After he went out Tahlvik picked up the radio set Matson had brought him. The same model as those given to Petrie and Shepherd. He sat down and began to turn the tuning dial slowly. He had already given instructions that all other high frequency wavelengths should close down for the afternoon and now, as he turned the knob, he switched from one set of atmospherics to another.

Then he heard the snatch of a voice and moved the knob back a fraction.

' – keep this line open. I would like to remain in contact.'

'Patience, brother. All is cool. We'll be away in just a few hours now. Out.'

Petrie's voice. The other must have been Shepherd. Tahlvik made a note of the wavelength and continued until he reached the end. He retraced the entire waveband. Then he stopped. 'You dumb idiot!' he said aloud.

His search had been for another wavelength. Petrie to lookout. But the commando had been spotted and the news relayed to the Boeing *before* the radio had been delivered to the hi-jackers. They had to have their own radio, operating on a different frequency entirely. They wanted these sets to allow their voices to travel the twelve miles from the airport to the besieged house. They obviously brought their own to contact their look-out who had to be within a few hundred yards at most.

Tahlvik slammed the set down and sat staring at it a long time. His thoughts were interrupted by the intercom.

'Where's this jack?' Petrie's voice and it sounded impatient.

'On its way,' Tahlvik said.

'You said that half an hour ago, Tahlvik.'

'It's still on its way,' he replied.

'How long does it take to repair all the wheels?'

'How should I know?' Tahlvik said.

'Because, Colonel, you are sitting in the middle of the air-port,' Petrie replied. 'You are surrounded by experts. Now come on, let's not try this casual routine. It will get you no-where, except nearer to the reputation of the soldier who pro-voked the biggest massacre of innocent people since the war.'

Tahlvik felt a quick flush of anger claw at his stomach. Here was a criminal facing him with the same arguments to let him get away with his crime as the authorities! Bernhard on one side, Petrie on the other. Both telling him that unless he did what they demanded he would have history against him. As if he weren't aware of the consequences. The television com-mentator chiding him with ill-concealed jibes at military procedures with an encore from Mrs Palmer telling him he ought to get out there himself instead of risking the lives of others. What, he wondered, was Palmer himself thinking? He looked and sounded the kind of man to advise him to do what he thought best. It was regrettable that, in moments of stress everyone looked out for their own reputations, their own situation; no one consulted those being threatened.

What were the odds? That Shepherd would kill Palmer and the housekeepers – very great indeed. Shepherd bore all the hallmarks of the fanatic despite his literacy. An ordinary man doesn't penetrate the heart of another country with a couple of popguns, seize prominent citizens and ransom them first of all for political demands, then for his own safety. Shepherd wasn't in it for money. Asking for ten million kroner – that was understandable. It was easy. You could pay crooks like that in stage money and they probably wouldn't spot the difference. But to risk everything to secure the freedom of others, there lay a different kind of person. Someone who never joked, never bluffed. Someone you took seriously and decided to fight at your peril. Back at the siege he had been prepared, albeit reluctantly, to accept the official view that the demands of the gunmen should be granted. Not for a moment had he contemplated a rush on the house. He had never doubted that all he would have found was a floor littered with corpses.

But what about Petrie? Denver says he and his men are neither cranks nor fools. But how fanatical are they? He remembered the overwhelming relief that passed through him when he saw the commando, caught like a cat in the pantry, released by the hi-jacker. Shepherd would have shot him without blinking. A warning to others. But Petrie? Petrie had called through and told him that the *next* one who tried anything would be shot. Would he go that far?

On the other hand it appeared that Petrie, realising his friends were going to fall into a trap, had calmly boarded the first flight out of London to Oslo, hi-jacked it as it landed and was holding it to ransom. The warning about the explosives could be a bluff but with a hundred civilians under his thumb he could afford to bluff. No one was prepared to question if there were bombs aboard or not. He knew that. Yet, once again, here was a man ready to risk his own life in order to secure the release of others. In wartime he would have been showered with medals. What greater love can a man show than to lay down his life for a friend and so on.

Tahlvik traced the outline of his pocket recorder, now stopped, and thought how quickly warfare had changed in the last few years. His peace-keeping missions had been confined to separating the races and tribes who fought each other for the old reasons; for land, property, for the control of the government. Once one of the sides had succeeded, he had watched them revert to the malpractices of the old. *Plus ça change* – not so today. These people, the Shepherds and Petries, might well go the way of the Robespierres and the Marats, they might well feel the pull of absolute power, the inability to stop snowballing towards a repetition of history that absolute power always seems to bring in its wake. But they fought differently. In the old days, once their dropping zone had been discovered, Shepherd and his people would have been written off. They would take up one corner on some roll of honour and probably receive an annual toast at a soldiers' reunion. But no self-respecting soldier would set up an operation to rescue them that would put them all at such risk. Heroism in the past was based on a mixture of schoolboy bravado plus a lack of imagination. The soldier who stood up and shot his machine gun from the hip while advancing on the entire Wehrmacht never considered he would die. He had probably read about such goings-on in a comic once. Shepherd and his like fully considered death; considered and dismissed it. And they had not read about their kind of warfare in comics. Their kind was new and so were their objectives. They wanted to destroy the government, not merely take it over. That was what made them so dangerous and ultimately that was also what made them so successful. Transport your war on to neutral territory and the chances are that you will win. And if you are caught, the chances are even greater that you will be released. Because sooner or later another gang will arrive to spring you from prison, and a third, if need be, will come to rescue them. So it goes until people yearn to live in peace and will agree to anything simply to be afforded the privilege of doing so.

Tahlvik knew he had no support anywhere for resistance. What would be said if he was successful? If, by some miracle as yet not evident, he managed to wean the hi-jackers from the 'plane, the gunmen from the Ambassador – what would be the reaction? He could hear it now. 'Damned irresponsible, Tahlvik. You gambled the lives of hundreds of people. Could have gone wrong. Just lucky we aren't all standing up in court trying to explain we didn't mean it.'

There was no way he could ultimately win. On the other hand if he pressed down that intercom switch, instructed the police to let Shepherd and his men come here, and put them aboard the aircraft, he would probably be given the Nobel Peace Prize. Commendations for exerting restraint on the natural impulses of a professional soldier. One short sentence into that machine at his elbow –

He made no move. Although he was helpless unless he found their look-out, although he knew it would take hours to locate him, something prevented him reaching out to order surrender.

Instead the intercom spoke to him. It was Matson's voice from upstairs. 'Colonel Tahlvik?'

'Yes?'

'I have Henry Bernhard on the line. He is most anxious to speak to you.'

'I'll bet he is,' Tahlvik muttered. He thought a moment, pondered the reaction if he left Bernhard on the end of a dead line. 'Transfer the call, please.'

A moment later his telephone rang and he picked it up. 'Hello,' he said.

'Tahlvik?' The voice was distant and blurred. Tahlvik realised Bernhard was speaking on a car telephone.

'Yes, speaking.'

'Colonel,' Bernhard shouted against the static, 'why have the gunmen not yet arrived at the airport?'

'The aircraft still needs lengthy repairs –' Tahlvik began but Bernhard cut in:

'I cannot hear you. I'm speaking from my car. Please raise your voice –'

Tahlvik grinned quickly to himself and *lowered* his voice. 'The problem is,' he said, 'the wheels. They blew out on landing and it is reckoned it will take at least –'

'Tahlvik, I can't hear you,' Bernhard yelled, his own voice almost deafening. 'I have just been told you risked the life of the passengers by sending one of your men out to storm the 'plane. Is this true?'

'Could you speak up?' Tahlvik said, hearing every word. 'We seem to be on a bad line.'

'I said, why did you –' Then everything dissolved in a loud crackle and Tahlvik pulled the receiver from his ear. He switched down the intercom.

'Matson, can you hear this?' he asked.

'Yes, Colonel,' Matson replied. 'I think he's heading this way and is going through the road tunnel. Perhaps it might not be wise to hang up.'

'Perhaps not. Thank you,' Tahlvik said.

Then Bernhard's voice returned, flailing through the interference. 'I'm on my way to you now,' he shouted. 'Arrange to be available in twenty minutes. Can you hear me?'

'Only just,' Tahlvik said. 'Can you repeat?'

'I will be there in twenty minutes –' Bernhard said, emphasising each word. He hadn't finished when Tahlvik broke in with:

'Good, I will look forward to seeing you.' And hung up.

The tunnel. He was nearer than twenty minutes. The tunnel –

A germ of an idea was born. Quickly he moved to the door and opened it. The guard, burly and impassive stood outside.

'You have your orders?' Tahlvik asked.

'Yes, sir,' the man replied, standing to attention.

'Which are?'

'Not to let anyone in your room unless you say so, sir.'

'Good,' Tahlvik said. 'The place is swarming with journalists. Some of them are pretty smart, they'll do anything to get a bit of copy for their papers. I want you to be particularly on the alert.'

'I will, sir, don't worry.'

'They might try and get in to see me,' Tahlvik said. 'They'll give you all kinds of excuses. Probably try and tell you they're the King or someone. Don't be misled.'

The man cracked his knuckles. 'Not me, sir.'

Tahlvik nodded and returned to his desk, closing the door. He called on the intercom for Donner and a minute later his tough frame appeared in the doorway. The guard looked over Donner at Tahlvik who said it was all right.

'We have to find this look-out,' Tahlvik said, facing the window again.

'Yes,' Donner answered. Tahlvik looked back at him.

'Any ideas?'

'Let's assume the look-out exists,' Donner said.

'Let's.'

'We could be wrong.'

'Let's assume he exists,' Tahlvik said. 'Now what?'

'He was put down to warn those inside the 'plane of any approach that they themselves couldn't see.'

'Or any kind of activity elsewhere in the airport they'd want to know about,' Tahlvik said.

'Possible, Nils,' Donner said. 'But if I were in there,' he pointed to the Boeing, 'I'd want to know what was going on round my back. Where someone could reach out and grab me unawares. I wouldn't be all that concerned with the outer perimeter. What could we do there? Station a few tanks, some mortars. So what? If we were thinking of a frontal attack, we'd have blasted the aircraft off the tarmac by now.'

'What's your point?' Tahlvik said.

'My point is that I arrived in an armoured car,' Donner replied. 'The lookout didn't see it. If he had, you would have had a squawk from Petrie about bringing up the army.'

'So?'

'So we drive that APC round and round until they *do* spot it,' Donner said.

Tahlvik frowned. 'Why, for heaven's sake?'

'Because if we play our cards very tight,' Donner said, 'the look-out will give his own position away. We need to drive the APC in specific areas that give a limited view on to the airfield. Keep it well out of sight of the 'plane. That way, as soon as Petrie gets on the blower and tells us to stop playing with fire, we can narrow down the area we have to search for his look-out. Suppose he's on that side of the field – ' Donner swept an arm in an arc to the left of the window.

'Right, we can drive the car behind these buildings, keep the terminal blocks between it and the Boeing but let it be seen from all those buildings on that side. He'll see it, report and once we hear Petrie complain, we'll know he's up there somewhere.'

Tahlvik scanned the left hand side of the field. 'Can we drive it round without Petrie himself seeing it?'

'I think so,' Donner said. 'He can't see anything this side of the Tower.'

Tahlvik pressed down the intercom switch: 'Are you up there, Matson?' he asked.

'Yes, Colonel.'

'I need a large-scale map of the airfield. One that shows the terminal buildings, hangars, maintenance sheds, everything.'

'I'll bring one down.' Tahlvik switched off.

'I can make the APC look pretty frightening with a few rifles,' Donner said.

'There's a squad of police somewhere armed to the teeth,' Tahlvik replied. 'Don't overdo it. We don't want Petrie to panic and put a match to everything.'

Someone knocked on the door. The guard put his head round. 'A Captain Barnes, sir.'

'Let him in.'

Barnes hurried in holding a long piece of paper, the kind used by telex machines.

'London has telexed the passenger list,' he said, handing the sheet over to Tahlvik. He watched the colonel flick his eyes down the names. Then he glanced up quickly.

'There's a Petrie down here.'

'Yes,' Barnes said. 'I've got London finding out if they have anything on someone with that name.'

'He used his own name?' Donner asked incredulously.

'Not necessarily,' Tahlvik said, scanning the rest of the names. 'He could have a passport taken from someone called Petrie and switched photos. Frank, he's got three others with him. See if London have any ideas. It means you have to prune down this list. Knock off anyone obviously not in the running. Women, children, there's a couple of Japanese here, a Brigadier Phillips. We're looking for three men aged around twenty-five, thirty-five, that bracket. Almost certainly English. It's a long shot but it just might produce something.'

Barnes nodded and took the list as Matson was let in by the guard. He was carrying a large, rolled up sheet of paper. As Barnes left, Matson unrolled the sheet on the desk, weighing down the corners with some coins.

'This is the best map of the airport. Shows just about everything.'

Tahlvik leaned his weight on his knuckles and bent over the map. He stared down at the diagrams. Unclipping a pen from a pocket, he glanced out of the window at the stranded Boeing, then placed the pen on the map where it was parked.

'There's our 'plane. We are here – ' he prodded a round diagram denoting the Control Tower. 'Now then, Matson, this is where we need your experience. Colonel Donner wants to drive an armoured personnel carrier around here and here – '

he waved his fingers over the roads behind the terminal buildings and maintenance sheds. 'However, it is essential the hi-jackers don't see him from the 'plane. We want to try and locate their look-out, who could be anywhere in this complex.'

'I see,' Matson said thoughtfully.

'These buildings –' Tahlvik pointed to several square marks behind and alongside the terminal buildings, 'are they solid enough, or tall enough to hide the vehicle from the Boeing? If they aren't, we're wasting our time. What we want is a route that gives everyone else around the airport a decent view of the APC except Petrie.'

Matson nodded and looked down at the map. He took out a felt pen and held it some moments while his eyes darted over the map. Finally he marked a space between two buildings behind the Tower.

'From here,' he said, 'the angle of vision is this –' He drew two lines in a large V-shape starting at the space between the buildings. The lines took in a large part of the west side of the airfield map. 'You see? Well away from the aircraft. Then there is here –' he marked another space between two squares marked 'Maintenance' and drew another V-shape across the map, some of which overlapped the first but then continued right across the wide spaces of the airfield itself, narrowly missing the pen representing the 'plane.

'Then I suppose this one would do –' Matson marked a third gap between buildings and drew a smaller V-shape which took in most of the terminal buildings behind them. 'You may have a problem getting to this one unobserved. Although you could take the perimeter road and cut across behind the snowbank.'

'What do you think, Donner?' Tahlvik asked, studying the black lines Matson had scored across the paper.

'Let's try it.'

'Thanks, Matson,' Tahlvik said. He even managed a weak smile.

'Good luck,' said the head of Airport Authority and left.

'You watch and I'll drive,' Donner grinned. Tahlvik grinned back.

'All right.' He held up his watch and synchronised the time with Donner's.

'Wait fifteen seconds at each space,' Tahlvik said. He took the pen up from the map and marked the crosses Matson had made: 1, 2, 3. 'Take them in that order. Get one of these radios from Matson and call me on this frequency.'

He showed Donner a mark on the tuning dial. 'Petrie and Shepherd are nowhere near it but just in case, say – what ? – Able Baker when you start, Charlie while you're waiting, and Dog when you move off to the next point.'

Donner nodded and moved to the door. 'What will you say if we hit the jackpot ?' he said.

Tahlvik grinned quickly. 'I'll probably be so relieved, I'll swear violently,' he said.

Donner left and Tahlvik returned to the map. To call it a long shot was an understatement. But it was all he had.

Outside his door the guard straightened as he heard footsteps clipping up the steps from below. Bernhard hurried into view. He stopped and looked at the guard. 'Is that Colonel Tahlvik's office ?'

There was a manner about the newcomer that immediately set the guard's teeth on edge. He looked him up and down. 'Who are you ?' he said.

Bernhard took the question as an answer to his own and moved forwards to enter the office. But the guard shot out a hand which rested, fingers splayed out, on Bernhard's chest. Bernhard took a step backwards. 'No one goes in there,' the guard said and pushed Bernhard back a pace.

'My name is Bernhard. I am from the Ministry of the Interior.'

'I don't care if you're King Canute,' the guard replied. 'I have my orders directly from Colonel Tahlvik and he says no one goes in there without his permission.'

'Then get it, you stupid – ' his words ran out.

The guard bristled a second, then relaxed, a smile appearing. 'I can't.'

'Why not?'

'I'm not supposed to leave this spot.'

Bernhard took a quick step forward. The guard's fists came up quickly.

'Try it,' he said, almost under his breath, 'I've always wanted to punch one of you people.'

Bernhard paused, thought better of it. Then he looked up the stairs and hurried up towards the Control Tower, watched by a triumphant guard.

'You don't fool me,' the guard called after him.

Bernhard stopped and looked down.

'You're a journalist,' the guard smiled. 'I know. I was warned about your kind by Colonel Tahlvik. Ministry of the Interior!'

Bernhard raised his eyes in a silent exclamation and continued up the steps.

Inside his office Tahlvik waited. A match-box lay on the map ready to make its tour from points 1 to 2 to 3, imitating the armoured personnel carrier.

Waiting was something Tahlvik could do without. It gave him time to think of questions he would prefer to remain unasked. Suppose they flushed the look-out from his hiding place – what then? How could he manoeuvre a group of commandos towards and on to the aircraft? He knew he could never try the rear approach again, nor use the entry beneath the pilot's cabin. Petrie was clever, he had proved that. He would be watching the hatch door from above all the time. In any case, Tahlvik thought, he would never ask Denver to risk his neck a second time.

Then there was Bernhard. Probably in the airport already. Bernhard who had the muscle to command him to stop any further attempts at resistance. Bernhard who had already, three hours ago, given him explicit instructions about yielding to their demands. Bernard who could, with one telephone call, have both himself and probably Polson suspended from duty for – what? So far the operation had consisted of making faltering steps into an increasingly dark tunnel.

Tunnel. Bernhard was certainly not going to like the way he had exploited the tunnel as an excuse to mishear the instructions thirty minutes ago. The tunnel . . .

The intercom buzzed. 'Yes?'

'Matson, Colonel. The jack has arrived. It's just passed the main gates.'

'Hold it back,' Tahlvik said. 'Don't let it get anywhere near the tarmac, not for the moment.'

'Very good.'

'Oh, and Matson – '

'Colonel?'

'Keep off the intercom for a while. I'm expecting a call from Petrie. Switch me through direct to the Boeing.'

'Will do.'

What was it he had been thinking about? The tunnel . . . Again he was interrupted by an eruption of squeaks from the two-way radio set. He picked it up and pressed the speaker button.

'Hello.'

'Able Baker.'

Tahlvik stood up, holding the set. 'Ready, Able Baker,' he said as he stooped over the airport map. Thirty seconds ticked by before the set spoke again:

'Charlie.'

Tahlvik picked up the match-box and placed it on the first cross marked by Matson. Holding his watch up in front of his face, he waited as the second hand covered a quarter segment. Any reaction from Petrie over the intercom would mean his look-out was holed up in any of the buildings on the west side of the airport.

'Dog.'

Donner's voice broke through his thoughts and Tahlvik brought down his watch. There was still a chance the message might be delayed and come through. He kept the match-box in place until Donner's voice crackled through on the set again.

'Able Baker.'

Tahlvik moved the match-box to the cross marked with a 2.

'Charlie.'

He held the watch up before his eyes and the second hand crawled haltingly round the dial. 'Dog.'

Tahlvik's stomach turned over with disappointment. It wasn't going to work, they had miscalculated entirely. The look-out must be somewhere else.

'Tahlvik! What the hell are you playing at!'

Petrie's voice spat through the intercom.

'Pull those troops back! If they get anywhere near us, I'll blow this 'plane up! You think I'm kidding? All right, then try me!'

Tahlvik wasn't listening. He grabbed the pen marking the position of the Boeing and began shading in the second of the long V-shapes Matson had scored across the map.

'You hear me, Tahlvik!' He reached over and switched down the intercom: 'I hear you Petrie. I'm moving them back now.' Picking up the two-way radio set he placed it next to his lips and spoke the most obscene military phrase he could think of, then returned to the map. Donner's voice replied, 'Roger.'

The shaded area took in most of the open airfield. The only building it encompassed was at the widest end of the V and they were almost a mile away on the farthest side of the perimeter. Frowning, Tahlvik picked up the map and took it to the window. He glanced from the diagram to the field outside.

There was nothing down there. Except – he dropped the map and his eyes narrowed as he peered downwards.

Off to the right, less than seventy yards from the Boeing, stood a line of private aircraft. Single- and twin-engined light-weight 'planes used by businessmen to hop fifty, a hundred miles. One or two had fluttered in to land since the Boeing had arrived. They all faced the hi-jacked 737 in a neat line. Because

91

they were such a familiar sight, Tahlvik had hardly seen them as he looked out his window. It wasn't possible their man was in one of *them* – ? 'The cheeky bastard!' he exclaimed aloud, and his tone held a considerable amount of awed admiration.

CHAPTER FIFTEEN

A single-engined Cessna fluttered down through the grey light of mid-afternoon and ran in towards the line of parked private aircraft. Touching down daintily, the machine ran lightly along the airstrip reserved for smaller 'planes. The pilot taxied, turned and stopped at one end of the line.

Keeping the engine running he reached for his radio. 'I can't see him,' he said.

Watching from his office below the Control Tower Tahlvik told the pilot to cut his engines and park.

'You have seven 'planes to investigate,' Tahlvik said. 'No one could sit in any of them and not be seen. Get out, go through the usual procedure for parking and try and spot him.'

The pilot acknowledged and switched off. He cut the engine and the propeller reduced its revolutions with a singing whine.

He was reaching for the catch to open his door when one of the other aircraft suddenly roared into life. Turning at the noise, he saw the pilot of a 'plane parked three places along the line sit upright from a cramped position below the line of the windows and let in the throttle.

On board the Boeing the small radio set held by Pete transmitted a terse message: 'George here! They've rumbled me! Be seeing you. Out.'

Petrie ran to a window and saw his look-out move his 'plane forwards, bumping over the frozen turf to the take-off strip.

'Christ! What happens now?' Pete said.

'Shut up!' Petrie snapped. Then he looked back at the line of 'planes as the newly-arrived Cessna restarted its engine.

The look-out skidded along the tarmac and rose unsteadily into the air. The Cessna followed in less of a hurry, keeping a steady course.

Petrie swore silently, then hurried into the pilot's cabin. He snatched the microphone from Denver. 'Tahlvik!' he snapped.

Tahlvik's voice answered blandly: 'Tahlvik here.'

'O.K. so you got rid of the look-out. Big deal. Now just where do you think that has got you? You reckon without him we're screwed. Tell me how. Tell me how you're even one per cent better off than before. I tell you, try sending another man from the rear and we'll see him. Try sending him up through the hatch and he'll get his head blown off. I'm not in the habit of repeating myself, Tahlvik, but this time I'll make an exception. At five-thirty, if we don't have our men from the Ambassador's house plus a new set of tyres plus permission to take off, I'll blow up the whole lot of us. Then there'll be no one for you to play soldiers with, will there?'

In the office, Tahlvik smiled to himself. For the first time Petrie sounded angry. Almost frightened.

'I hear you, Petrie,' he replied.

Petrie slammed the microphone back into Denver's hand and moved out of the cabin. Pete had heard him lay into Tahlvik on the radio and he smiled.

'That'll show him not to piss about,' he said.

Petrie turned on him, his face livid with anger. 'You get back to your post!' he shouted. 'You don't seem to appreciate one rather important fact – this colonel they've got is good. He's more than that, he's bloody good. How in hell did he rumble George? He didn't get anywhere near him. It's impossible to look into the 'plane from the Control Tower. Every time there's been a landing George got down on the floor. How did he do it?'

The question was directed at no one in particular. Petrie looked at Pete. 'Bear one thing in mind,' he said, under his breath, 'Tahlvik is good and he's up to something. So keep your eyes open. Tell the others.'

In the Tower, Tahlvik told his pilot to keep the look-out 'plane in sight. 'He's bound to come down soon,' he said. 'I want to know where.'

The pilot acknowledged then tucked the radio away as he climbed up through the low clouds hanging over the airport. His quarry disappeared for some moments before re-appearing again fifty yards to his right. He was zig-zagging through the clouds trying to shake off his pursuer. Tahlvik's pilot soon realised that the man ahead was an experienced flyer. Opening the throttle he began to climb, trying to get above the thick bank of cloud which prevented him from keeping the course set for him by the 'plane in front.

Up he went, the engine straining with the effort. The moisture in the cloud spattered the windscreen. He turned on the wipers but his visibility was reduced even further.

Then he was out of the bank. He straightened a hundred feet above it and began tilting the wings to give him a view below. There was no sign of the other aircraft. Where the hell had it gone? Not down again, surely!

The pilot put the Cessna into a long downward curve and plunged among the clouds again. If the other one were below, he would be seen from the ground. But that would present few problems since the ground surrounding Fornebu was desolate. Few people lived down there and those who did would hardly take much notice of a small aeroplane passing overhead.

He emerged at 900 feet into the darkening grey light and peered round, craning his neck. Then he saw him. The other 'plane was cruising just under the level of the clouds, occasionally stitching a path through some underhanging wisps. He was moving in a straight south-easterly direction. Tahlvik's pilot radioed through to the Control Tower that he had the man in sight. Control replied that both of them were showing on the radar scanner but were approaching the outer rim of the circular screen.

'We're trying the airforce,' Matson said, 'to see if they can track him further on their bigger screens. Meanwhile, keep on his tail in case they can't.'

The pilot acknowledged and switched off. He increased speed and altitude until he was a quarter of a mile behind the look-out 'plane and two hundred feet higher. This took him into considerable cloud and for long periods of half a minute or more he lost sight of his quarry. However, when he re-emerged it was still there, flying dead straight, giving the impression he was heading for a specific point. He seemed to be unaware of his follower and kept to a regular speed. They continued like this for five miles and the Cessna pilot settled comfortably back for what appeared to be a leisurely ride.

Suddenly everything changed. The look-out pilot opened the throttle and without warning made a left turning into a bank of cloud. The Cessna was taken completely by surprise. It swung clumsily round in pursuit climbing a little as the pilot had seen the 'plane in front hit the cloud at an upward angle.

Once inside the bank the Cessna pilot knew his quarry had been waiting for just this chance to escape. He floundered in a dense, grey mass of condensation, much thicker than the previous formations he had passed through. It was like trying to find a pinch of salt in a ball of cotton wool. The wipers raced back and forth over the windscreen but were of little help. Running constantly through his mind was the fear of a collision. Control hadn't called through. Meaning the two aircraft were well off the range of the airport scanner.

He began to feel a crushing, claustrophobic fear as the Cessna pushed and flailed through the cloud bank. No one flies by choice in this kind of formation, especially when there is another machine somewhere near by. If they should collide it would happen in a split second. No warning, no anticipatory noise or vision. Just bang and then silence. He brought the stick back and the Cessna roared upwards steeply, straining to find clear skies again. Up he went, 100, 200 yards before the cloud thinned and the bright rays of the sun, low on the horizon, flooded in from the rear.

Of the other 'plane there was no sign. He flew zigzagging above the bank from which he had emerged but either the other man had descended again or was not as terrified of the cloud as he was.

He picked up his microphone and reported he had lost the look-out aircraft. 'Come back to base,' a voice replied.

Bitterly disappointed, blaming himself for being caught unawares, then for having had his nerve tested in the cloudbank and found wanting, the Cessna pilot swung round and headed home.

CHAPTER SIXTEEN

The little 'plane hovered over the dead, cold landscape searching for a couple of hundred yards that would let it come down and settle. Below, the bleakness of the terrain, covered for almost two months with snow which was re-frozen every twenty-four hours by the blistering cold winds coming in from the sea, made the pilot shiver involuntarily.

He dropped another fifty feet until he was skimming the tops of the trees. Finally he selected a spot; a long, thin stretch between a snow ridge and a deserted but modern road. No point in coming down only to freeze to bloody death, he thought. I need transport to get back to civilisation. If there was such a thing as civilisation in this God-forsaken spot. He hadn't flown over any sign of life at all, human or animal. But his fuel gauge had dropped and leaving the airport to go south-east, rather than head back to where he had arrived in the country, had screwed up the on-going arrangements completely. Still, that's what he had been told to do and you didn't mess about with these characters.

He braced himself for a rocky touch down and brought the nose of the aircraft gently down to face the onrush of a rock-hard open field. The wheels touched, screeched and raised in protest at the hardness of impact. They came down a second then a third time before allowing the 'plane above them to settle down for a two hundred yard bone-shaking ride. The pilot held on to the stick with both hands and clamped his jaws tight shut. The 'plane slewed from side to side as it slowed but using the brakes intelligently he managed to come to a shuddering halt without twisting sideways and inviting a roll-over crash stop.

He killed the engine and sat for some moments without

moving. What had he to do? The radio. Leaning backwards he pulled out the small two-way radio he had used to speak to Pete in the Boeing. Then he opened the door and jumped down. The radio fell to the ground. He brought up a boot and stamped heavily down, crunching the set to pieces. Then he picked it up, walked round the tail of the 'plane and hurled the wreckage as far as he could into the snowbank.

Squinting into the distance he picked out the road which ran in from the coast. He began to run towards it, but slowed down when he realised how slippery the earth below him had become. It was like running on marbles. A broken ankle now and the next time he would be allowed to walk around free would be when he was about sixty. So he picked his way carefully towards the road, holding his arms out on either side to steady his balance.

He reached the road and looked in both directions. He had the choice of going to the coast – the road had to lead somewhere – or moving inland until something came along to give him a lift. The coast was nearer. There had to be *some*one living there. Heading inland he could travel for hours and still end up on the top of a mountain. He chose the southerly route and began to jogtrot along the side of the newly laid tarmac.

How had they rumbled him? As he ran he tried to work out what had gone wrong. His last message to the Boeing was to tell them about the tank and the soldiers. They couldn't have found the wavelength and if they had, they would have spent hours trying to figure out where he was speaking from. Two private 'planes had come down while he had been there, only two, and each pilot had moored, locked up and gone while he had been crouching on the floor of the cockpit. There was no way he could have been seen. Yet the third one to land had taken too long to cut his engines. And he had seen the pilot use the radio. Nobody uses the radio at that stage of landing. No one looks round at the rest of the moored aircraft as this one had done. No, he had been right to make a dash for it.

The bloke had been sent to get him, that much was proved by the way he followed him up. But how did they know he was there?

The pilot was not a man for introspection and he shrugged off the failure and stopped trying to find reasons for it. His problem was now simple: to get the hell out of Norway and return to England. He had a passport and he had money. Maybe there were boats on the coast that could take him if not all, then part of the way back to Oslo to pick up a ferry.

A car appeared behind him in the distance, a mile up the arrow-straight road. He heard it when it was about a quarter of a mile away. He stopped, panting clouds of steam into the thin air, and waited. Stroke of luck, he thought. Could be miles to the sea yet. As the car approached he stepped out into the road and held up an arm, drawing his thumb in the direction the car was travelling. He heard it change down and grinned. It was going to stop for him. As it drew alongside he stood, hands on hips, trying to regain his breath. 'You go far?' a voice said in English.

He looked inside. The car held three men, two up front, one behind.

'Want to get to the sea,' he said between breaths. 'Is it far?'

'No. Get in.' The man in the rear leaned over and opened the door. The pilot climbed in gratefully.

'Blimey, it's cold,' he said, closing the car door. Then he looked at the man beside him. The car started off rapidly. Something told him all was not quite as it should be. Why was the man next to him smiling in that strange way? Why was the car picking up speed, going much faster than when it had approached him?

'Where did you leave your aeroplane?' the man beside him said quietly.

He started. The man in the passenger seat turned and showed a gun in his hand.

'What's all this, then?' he said weakly, already knowing the answer.

The man next to him brought out a wallet. Opening it up he showed a police identification card.

'What do you want me for?' he said, even more weakly. 'I mean, it's not a crime to hitch-hike in this country, is it?'

The man by his side said nothing. But he did smile quite broadly.

CHAPTER SEVENTEEN

The police station was heated and well insulated. The pilot had reason to be thankful for this since he had been seated in front of a glowing radiator for the best part of an hour with only a blanket to cover his naked body. They had told him to strip and his clothes had disappeared into another room where the Inspector, the man who had sat next to him in the car, had proceeded to make a series of telephone calls. His demand, which had become diluted into a request, for a cup of tea, was answered with a mug of thick black cocoa. His protestations about the way a foreigner was treated in this country went unobserved.

Finally the Inspector returned. He carried the pilot's clothes. He was a small, mournful-looking man but even his spaniel features didn't quite conceal a look of quiet triumph.

'When I've made my official complaint to the authorities,' the pilot said, drawing the blanket round him and trying to ignore the fact he was unclothed, 'your feet won't touch the ground. A bloke can't go for a quiet spin without being clobbered by the bleeding law. Nice little run into the country-side and bam! Next thing you know, you're in the nick. Wait till my Embassy hears about this, matey, you'll be in it up to here — '

He let go of the blanket to rest a finger against his neck. By doing so the blanket fell to the floor. The pilot reddened and stooped quickly to pick it up and cover himself.

The Inspector smiled. 'I think your Ambassador is temporarily indisposed,' he said. 'But surely you must know about that.'

'I don't know anything of the sort,' the pilot replied.

'Can you not read?'

"'Course I can.'

'The papers have been printing the account of the siege of the British Ambassador's house for the last two days,' the Inspector said mildly.

'I'm surprised you haven't heard at least *something* about it. It's been on the radio, television – where have you been recently?'

The pilot sniffed. 'Oh, that,' he said. 'Yeah, well, I mean I knew about that, didn't I?'

The Inspector was not acquainted with cockney syntax. 'That's what we are trying to discover,' he said.

'What did you pick me up for? And why did you take my clothes. What's going on here? Some kind of mental torture, is it? I know something about the Germans, you know. About how the Gestapo used to interrogate people after making them sit around in the nude. Supposed to destroy their dignity, make them give in quick.'

'I never heard that,' the Inspector said, sounding intrigued. 'Is that what really happened?'

The pilot didn't reply. The Inspector placed the bundle of clothes on a table and sat down beside it.

'Where do you come from?' he asked quietly.

'I don't have to answer your questions,' the pilot said. He had once been told his constitutional rights but he wasn't quite sure if they applied in other countries.

'Then let me answer them for you,' the Inspector replied.

The pilot's stomach turned over. When policemen talk calmly and when they smile a lot, it means they know all the answers before they ask the questions. And this man was doing both. 'You come from Bournemouth in England.'

Yes, the pilot thought. He knows the answers all right. 'Where's Bournemouth?' he said aloud but not with much thrust behind his words.

The Inspector picked up the man's windcheater jacket. 'Borrowing something from your Sherlock Holmes, I noticed your coat was bought at a store in Bournemouth.' He displayed the tag on the inside, then picked up the pair of boots on the table. 'The same applies to these.'

'Someone gave them to me.'

'You aren't going to be difficult, are you?' the Inspector asked.

'Not me, mate,' the pilot replied. 'I'm all for international brotherhood and universal bloody peace.'

'I have spoken to the British police. It didn't take them long to discover how many pilots with a criminal record lived in Bournemouth.'

'Criminal record? I've never been so insulted – I'll sue you for slander!'

Well, it was worth a try, the pilot thought as he spluttered. Better than sitting there and just taking it from this weasel.

'Yes,' the Inspector went on. 'And not a very good one either – '

He glanced at a piece of paper he was holding. 'Mr Rawlings.'

The pilot gave up. He drew the coarse blanket tight round his shoulders and sunk his chin into his chest. Screw the lot of them.

'You have been convicted, I see, for passing useless cheques, fraud, demanding money with menaces and – '

The Inspector squinted at the paper with a crooked smile: ' – indecent exposure.'

He smiled again at the silent pilot.

'Perhaps the last offence was committed so that you could show people you were not entirely without substance.'

'Very funny.'

'There is one aspect of your career, however, that intrigues me more than this,' the Inspector continued.

'What's that?'

'It says here you were arrested in the Persian Gulf having flown an aircraft illegally from India. An aircraft which had previously been involved in the gold smuggling trade across the Indian Ocean.'

104

'I never got done for that,' the pilot protested hotly. 'Ask anyone.'

'Exactly,' the Inspector answered. 'That is what intrigues me.'

The pilot suddenly went very quiet.

'Your early criminal career, when you were searching around to find the crime at which you were best, ended four years ago. Presumably you decided against fraud, extortion and even flashing, as a suitable method to earn your fortune and took to the air. After regular visits to prison since the age of fifteen, you turn over a new leaf. You are no longer convicted. But last year you are arrested on what seems to be convincing evidence. You land in Dubai – I presume some of those four missing years were spent learning to fly? – with an aircraft logged out of Goa. Now, Mr Rawlings, I will tell you something. There is a great deal of boring, routine work in the police force. Much of one's life is spent looking for needles which do not exist in haystacks that are miles in circumference. But occasionally, just occasionally, one stumbles across something which exercises the brain. Which provides a shot of adrenalin to revive one's spirits and make one say to oneself, "Perhaps the job is worth sticking at, after all." I am most grateful to you. You have ended a long run of tedious months during which none of the cases under my scrutiny held the slightest interest. But here is a puzzle, a genuine riddle: how is it that a man whose background is one of petty crime for which he is singularly ill-equipped; how is it that a man who even manages to get himself arrested for indecent exposure, suddenly raises his sights to the gold smuggling business? And not only that – having done so, how is it, when he is caught, that he can successfully talk his way out of a charge? I must confess, Mr Rawlings, the transformation in you has caught my imagination. Tell me how you did it.'

The pilot pulled a face and dropped his head again. The Inspector smiled and leaned back in his chair.

CHAPTER EIGHTEEN

A figure wearing a track-suit and with a towel covering the back of his neck, the ends tucked into the front of the top of the suit, trotted quickly round the perimeter road of the airport.

As he ran, Tahlvik listened to the playback of the events of the day recorded into his miniature cassette. The box rested in an inside pocket and a wire ran up and into his right ear.

The crisp air revived him like a cold shower. Two days of sitting down either in his car or in offices had slowed down his circulation until he could almost feel the sluggishness of the blood through his veins. But now his heart was pumping fiercely at 90 and the tingling had returned to his skin, two sensations he looked forward to after a week behind his desk. He had been chairbound for three years, ever since his promotion to colonel and as far as he could see, would spend the remainder of his career sitting down. The price paid for success. His happiest days as a soldier were long past: Korea after the cease fire, and the farcical peace talks which went on for years. He had liked Korea. The extremes of climate, the gentleness of the people. Wars were still simple in those days, the issues were uncomplicated and the opposing forces looked different. It was *them* against *us*, East versus West, capitalism fighting communism. Korea was a Holy War, the first to be waged by the United Nations; a call to all freedom-loving peoples to join together and put the infidel to the sword. Or so it seemed. Nobody reneged during the war. Unlike Vietnam, nobody reappraised the reason for fighting year after year among the barren hills of the North. It was an old-style war, a well-made war with a beginning, middle and end in that order.

The Congo was quite different, the first of the savage civil conflicts to evolve from independence. Far worse than Cyprus where the enemy were the British; only after they went did Greek set about Turk with any real enthusiasm. He remembered the decimated villages in the Congo, the unbelievable cruelties men perpetrated on their own kind. No, he hadn't enjoyed the Congo. There was no clear distinction between *them* and *us*. You can't referee a fight if you cannot distinguish the opponents.

Which was the case here today. As he jogtrotted round the perimeter path out of sight of the Boeing, Tahlvik considered the possibility that he was getting too old for the game. As soon as you say to yourself that you no longer understand the modern world, then it usually means you are over the hill. But since the siege of the British Ambassador's house began over two days ago, he had struggled to find even the smallest part of the operation which he could, even if he did not condone it, at least understand.

There was nothing. Four gunmen threaten to murder three elderly people unless the British authorities release their friends who have been arrested on criminal charges. There is no question of bluff; the executions will take place if their demands are not met. The leader of the squad is a well-known anarchist responsible for murderous outrages against his own people for several years. For what reason? Presumably to destroy the political system under which he lives. The war is conducted against his own kind but on foreign soil, recent history having proved that perpetrators of this kind of operation stand a greater chance of success if they act in another country.

And the government of the neutral ground, where the war is fought, agree to let them go. Not in order to save the lives of the three elderly hostages, but in order to guarantee freedom from further trouble in their country in the future.

In such a war, who is *them* and who is *us*? The question

which used to be so simple to answer when countries fought each other – who is right and who is wrong – are now unanswerable. No one nowadays tears up a treaty or invades another's land, thus starting a chain of events which, when they end in a declaration of war, can get a seal of approval from the United Nations. At one time the fear was that with the advent of the atomic age, the next war would be so big it would be the last. But what has happened is the reverse. Warfare has become fragmented to such an extent that even brush-fire rows now seem big affairs. The Middle East produces old-fashioned battles played on what today seems a huge canvas, but Ireland is the best example of the modern war. There, men shoot their brothers in back alleys of small towns. This was the type of warfare Tahlvik knew that as a soldier, he must try to understand. He doubted his ability to do so.

So far he had avoided Bernhard, except for a brief moment when both were watching the radar scanner until the two white dots disappeared off the edge. He had cut Bernhard short by telling him he had to contact the airforce to track the look-out pilot's aircraft and the pursuing Cessna. He had almost run from the Control Room and returned to the office on the floor below where the guard prevented Bernhard advancing any farther. The airforce agreed, had already seen the dots on their own scanner and telephoned the map reference where the first dot had disappeared.

The police report would be interesting. He didn't expect the hi-jackers to capitulate simply because of the capture of one of their accomplices, but for the first time Tahlvik felt that some positive progress had been made. Only two and a half hours remained till the deadline. Until now there had been no kind of encouragement to persuade him to continue. At least the inevitable meeting with Bernhard would not be entirely one-sided.

He reached halfway round the perimeter and for a brief moment the distant Control Tower came into view as the snowbank ended. The stranded 737 looked like a toy at the distance, less intimidating than the view from his office.

Trotting on, his brain cleared as fresh blood coursed through his system. Several questions which had lain dormant or only half-formed during the dead, sleepless two days began to swim into focus.

How had four men boarded an aircraft carrying an arsenal of weapons ? What was even more bizarre – how, with such luggage, had they boarded a flight to a city where a siege had already been going on for two days ? London Airport hadn't yet replied but it was reasonable to suppose they were using magnetometers. Security machinery was a regular feature at Heathrow and had been for some years. But that was incidental. Supposing the system had become lax – it usually did on routes where trouble was not expected – the authorities would have to be criminally insane not to clamp down on passengers coming to Oslo since Sunday.

Yet here they were, trying to outwit four heavily armed men seated on a flight from London who had also carried enough explosives on board to blow the aircraft to pieces.

Then there was Petrie. A man known to Shepherd, travelling under a name which Shepherd recognised – using that name to book an air ticket. London had discovered one of the men holding Palmer was Shepherd. And yet they let Petrie slip out of the country, using his own name to board a flight to where Shepherd was holed up – someone was going to have to answer a great number of questions when this was over. Someone in the British Defence Ministry, some senior officer put out to pasture –

Someone probably very much like himself. Someone who, at this very moment, was following the situation in London and blaming his own lack of understanding for the mistakes he had made. Someone who doubted his ability to comprehend modern warfare, who said every time the papers carried news of another senseless airport massacre, that he was living in a different world to the one he knew and could cope with. He had already made his errors and created the present situation. As Tahlvik ran along the path towards the terminal buildings, he wondered if he would complete the errors which could send the present situation spinning into a final bloodbath.

CHAPTER NINETEEN

The hot water hit his tingling body like a million scalding needles and took his breath away. He held his face upwards into the force of the spray, an inch from the shower rose and the water drummed on his eyelids. Gasping, he turned and gave his back the same treatment.

The door to the shower-room opened and Barnes came in, carrying Tahlvik's clothes. He put them down on a bench. His hands also held some papers.

Tahlvik opened his eyes to reach for the soap and saw Barnes. 'Thanks, Frank.'

He began to scrub his body vigorously with the soap, the soft water creating a lather which ran in rivulets down the length of his body to the drain beneath his feet.

'I've heard from London,' Barnes began. He didn't sound enthusiastic.

'Oh yes?'

'Do you want to hear it?'

'Am I going to like it?'

'Not much,' Barnes replied.

Tahlvik smiled through the steam of the shower. 'Try me.'

'Well,' Barnes said, glancing at the papers in his hand, 'number one – London airport has had all its magnetometers going full blast, particularly for flights stopping here since Sunday.'

'I would have been amazed if they hadn't,' Tahlvik said.

'They've been carrying out their own investigations since they heard about the hi-jack,' Barnes said. 'At first they tried to say it was impossible. They asked us to check if the guns were real. They said plastic looked similar and if they hadn't fired one yet, how could we be absolutely certain – '

'Perhaps we should ask Petrie to shoot a passenger just for proof,' Tahlvik said.

He stepped out of the shower and reached for a towel. Like most Englishmen Barnes felt uncomfortable looking at a man who could walk around nude in front of him without embarrassment. He half turned so as not to stare directly at Tahlvik as he dried himself.

Tahlvik noticed the reaction and smiled to himself. 'That was "at first",' he said.

'What ?'

'You said London Airport said this "at first". But then – ?'

'Well, then I told them we had the pilot's word that the guns the men carried *were* real. They said the only answer was the weapons and explosives must have been placed aboard by one or two of the ground staff. A number of people have access to the aircraft while it is on the ground. Cleaners, caterers, dozens of people go on and off while the flight is prepared.'

'They aren't checked ?' Tahlvik asked, beginning to dress.

'Not as a rule, apparently. There are a few red faces in the airport at present because they ought to have clamped down on the Boeing from the moment it was scheduled for the Oslo flight.'

'And they didn't ?'

'They began to stammer a bit,' Barnes said. 'Reading between the "ums" and "ers", I'd say they didn't bother.'

'That is one solution,' Tahlvik said. 'Although I cannot say I place much faith in it.'

'Airports are full of people who can be got at,' Barnes said. 'Ask any smuggler.'

'Given time and preparation, yes,' Tahlvik replied, buttoning his shirt, 'but what happened in our case ? British Intelligence discovered where Shepherd and his men planned to bale out. Petrie found out they knew. So he rounds up three friends and climbs aboard the first flight to Oslo. You are asking me to believe there was someone in the airport who could ferry on guns and dynamite at the drop of a hat. Standing around with them in his pockets, waiting to be asked. I can't believe that.'

Barnes shrugged. What Tahlvik said made sense. 'How else was it done, then ?' he asked.

'I don't know, Frank,' Tahlvik said. 'I know I'm being difficult. You give me a perfectly feasible explanation and I knock it down without offering anything better.'

Barnes said nothing. Tahlvik finished dressing in silence. He turned to Barnes, ready to leave the shower room and found the Englishman gnawing his lip. Tahlvik realised that the silence had been caused by something Barnes wanted to say but for some reason found it hard to put into words.

'You began by saying "number one",' Tahlvik said. 'Is there a number two ?'

Barnes reluctantly handed over a telex sheet. Tahlvik read it, his frown increasing as he scanned the thirty-odd words printed on the paper.

He looked up. 'So Scotland Yard have known about Petrie for a couple of years,' he said. Then a pause. 'Well, well, well.'

He walked out of the shower room, his track-suit rolled up under an arm. Barnes followed him out. They left the staff quarters and walked across the compound towards the Control Tower.

Barnes was the first to break the silence between them. 'He must be rather smart,' he said lamely.

Tahlvik laughed quickly, amused at the British habit of falling back on understatement when their thoughts are in a mess.

'He must also be rather lucky,' he said. 'He travels under a name the police know about. Have known about for a couple of years. He walks through the tightest airport security check on to a flight to the country where his known friends are holding an Ambassador to ransom. He brings with him an armful of weapons and a bag of dynamite. Frank,' Tahlvik said as they entered the Control Tower and walked towards the lift, 'this man isn't just lucky. He's a walking bloody miracle!'

Barnes didn't answer. They rode to the floor below the Control Room and Tahlvik stepped out. He gave the hint to Barnes: 'If you see Colonel Donner upstairs,' he said, 'ask him to see me in the office.'

Barnes checked his steps out of the lift and stayed inside. The doors closed and he pressed the button for the Control Room.

Donner was there and he passed on the message. The colonel went down the steps and entered the office.

Tahlvik was back at the window. The light was beginning to fade outside. In an hour it would be dark. The jack was now in place below the Boeing and the arduous process of changing all the wheels under way. A movement at the door of the aircraft suggested the mechanics working with the jack were under constant supervision by one of the hi-jackers.

'You want to see me?' Donner said.

Tahlvik turned from the window. 'Where's Bernhard?'

'He was upstairs, but he left about twenty minutes ago.'

'Probably gone to fetch a firing squad,' Tahlvik smiled grimly.

'Time is running out,' Donner said, looking at his watch.

'Yes.'

'Are you going to give in?'

'What do you think I ought to do?'

'It doesn't matter what I think,' Donner said with an open smile. 'You only take your own advice.'

Tahlvik laughed. 'Perhaps that has always been my trouble,' he said.

He reached over to the intercom and pressed down the switch. 'Captain Denver –'

'Captain,' Tahlvik said quietly, 'let me speak to Petrie.'

'I'm here, Colonel,' Petrie's voice came on. 'What do you want?'

There was a long pause. 'Petrie,' Tahlvik said, 'your men will be released. They should be here within 45 minutes.'

Petrie didn't answer for a good five seconds and when he did, the relief was audible. 'Fine, Tahlvik.'

Tahlvik switched off the intercom. The room was plunged into a strange silence as he turned to look at Donner who stood rooted to the spot, unable to speak.

Then Tahlvik told him to sit down.

CHAPTER TWENTY

Petrie turned from the microphone towards Denver. 'He's agreed to release our friends,' he said, trying to disguise the flood of relief which surged through his body. He tried to sound calm, as if this was what he had always expected.

The news was received by Roper without any attempt to disguise his pleasure.

'Thank sweet Christ!' he said, leaning back and closing his eyes. Denver said nothing.

Petrie left the cockpit and told the passengers over the inter-com that they would shortly be allowed to leave. Nobody cheered. Exhaustion had set in half an hour ago; exhaustion coupled with fear, perhaps the most debilitating mixture of all. All that happened was that the mothers hugged their children and some of the men blew out their cheeks in a silent release of tension.

Pete called Shepherd on the two-way radio: 'Sunflower –'

'Sunflower here.'

'They have given in, Sunflower. You have been released. You will have safe conduct to the airport.'

Shepherd's voice came on the other end. 'We don't need safe conduct. We are bringing our hostages with us. Tell the authorities that we shall kill them all if there is any attempt to stop us. Out.'

Shepherd handed the set brusquely back to Mike. His face was set and none of the expected relief showed. The last hour in the house had been bad. Twice he had exploded with rage, once at Mike, then soon afterwards at Terry, both of whom had merely asked how things were going. Perfectly reasonable questions, but he had lost control. It was a bad mistake which could have proved fatal. Shepherd felt his stomach crawl with anxiety. Lack of sleep combined with the loss of control had produced a despair in him that filled him with a sense of doom. Never before had he experienced such a feeling. A great deal of his success in the past was due to his ability to overcome pessimism in others. People envied him his daring, marvelled at the way he could decide instantly to try something the police would never consider was possible. Each time he had proved himself right. It had all been so easy. Until today. Today was the first time the operation had gone seriously wrong. He should have felt grateful that someone had arrived to repair the damage. But he didn't. In a perverse way, he resented Petrie. Resented being told to stand by; resented having his questions left unanswered; resented having to wait upon someone else's convenience. So, when the news arrived that they were going to be freed, some of the sweetness of victory was absent. This was Petrie's victory, not his own.

He slipped his mask over his face and dipped under the curtain.

Palmer had his eyes closed but he opened them at once when Shepherd bobbed up beside him. 'We are going,' he said.

'What's happened?' Palmer asked.

'The colonel has agreed to let us go to the airport.'

'Colonel Tahlvik?'

'Yes.'

Palmer frowned. 'You are a lucky man,' he said. 'I would have bet on Tahlvik never giving in.'

'*We* are lucky?' Shepherd asked. 'Don't you include yourself in on the luck?'

Palmer didn't reply. The pain in his chest was severe now and each breath made it worse.

'Do you need a pill?' Shepherd asked, seeing how stiffly Palmer moved.

The Ambassador shook his head. 'Not for another hour.'

Shepherd moved round to the housekeepers. The woman was asleep, her face creased with worry as she slept. Her husband looked up at the mask and didn't react when Shepherd told him they were about to go.

Mike brought Eva and Terry down from their posts upstairs.

'I was beginning to think we weren't going to make it,' Terry said.

'We haven't, not yet,' Shepherd replied. 'They have a dozen ways they could stop us. Staying in here was the easy part. If any of you are feeling sleepy, put your head under the cold tap. You know the plan. We go in the minibus outside, same arrangements as before. Are all the parachutes aboard?'

He turned to Terry who nodded. 'Untie the Ambassador and the other two.'

While Eva unpicked the knots in the cord binding the couple's wrists, Mike unclipped the belts holding Palmer in his seat. The hostages climbed rockily to their feet. The woman cried out softly in pain and her husband sat her down again and began to massage her legs. Palmer shrugged off Eva's arm and walked stiffly through the curtain, yanking it aside. Shepherd picked up the phial of pills and put them in his pocket.

Beyond the gates of the house the crowds began to stir. They heard the news that the gunmen were shortly to come out and the journalists and the television cameramen kneaded their frozen, cramped joints to be ready for the exodus. The police started to push back the onlookers who were across the path leading out from the gates, shouting and waving their arms, swearing at those who were slow to move. The time had long passed for reason and goodwill. Everybody outside the house was irritable, angry and woolly-headed from the hours of waiting in the sub-zero weather and tempers flared several times before the journalists and the cameramen reluctantly moved back to new positions.

A few minutes later the main door opened and the cameras clicked and whirled as a man wearing a stocking mask and holding a revolver sprinted out and climbed up alongside the driver waiting in the minibus. He was followed by another holding Palmer, then a third and fourth each side of the housekeepers who hobbled slowly out and had to be helped up into the bus. The doors slammed shut and the driver started up the engine. It took several long bursts on the starter button before the engine sprang into life. The driver let in the clutch and the minibus slowly rolled down the incline towards the gates. As it passed through, the press corps and cameras dipped in unison to catch an eye-level glimpse of the occupants. Cameras flashed as the vehicle rolled out of the gates, turning to move towards the road. The police held back the spectators but couldn't prevent a number of hisses and shouts. One man waved a fist and yelled a few words close to the window of the bus as it passed by. No one inside moved an inch.

Soon the vehicle was free of the people and gathered speed, disappearing into the gathering gloom of the late afternoon.

CHAPTER TWENTY-ONE

'Colonel, the Inspector who arrested the look-out pilot has arrived.' The voice belonged to the airport guard at the main gate.

'I'll come down.'

Tahlvik glanced at his watch. At any moment Bernhard was going to burst through the door and tell him he was under arrest, suspended from duty or something of the sort and there would be nothing more he could do. Better stay out of doors as much as possible.

'I'll be gone ten minutes,' he told the guard, then hurried down the steps to the ground exit.

He drove along the straight road to the main gates and passed a police helicopter parked fifty yards inside the perimeter. The Inspector came out of the gate office and clicked his heels formally, holding out a hand. 'Schmidt.'

'I'm Colonel Tahlvik.'

'I thought it wise not to let them see a helicopter arrive,' Schmidt said, indicating the machine.

'You thought well,' Tahlvik said. Within five seconds he had formed an opinion of the man who faced him. Quiet, self-effacing, utterly reliable and a supreme professional. At the same time he looked as if he had never had either a square deal or a square meal in his life. One of nature's worriers. A quality essential in a policeman.

'You caught the pilot.'

'I caught *a* pilot,' Schmidt replied.

They walked slowly away from the main gates towards the helicopter.

'You didn't come all this way for a ride,' Tahlvik said. 'Nor to tell me face to face something you could have telephoned.'

'No.' Tahlvik allowed Schmidt to set his own pace to the conversation. And he wasn't going to be hurried.

'We discovered his identity,' Schmidt said. 'English. Name George Rawlings. A criminal record of middle-weight crimes ranging to the downright petty or farcical.'

'Any political sympathies?'

'Colonel Tahlvik,' Schmidt said, 'this man would not recognise a political belief if it bit him on the nose.'

'Why do you suppose he was hired for this job, then? The men holding the British Ambassador, the men holding the 'plane all belong to a political movement. They aren't here for money or to save their own skins. Why choose Rawlings for what was one of the riskiest jobs of the operation?'

'He can fly.'

'True,' Tahlvik nodded. 'As a matter of fact, the man we sent after him said he could fly like a dream.'

'There is your answer.'

'Part of it.' They strolled around the helicopter. Schmidt had something else to say but he wasn't going to waste it by bad timing.

'Rawlings's record is interesting,' he continued after a while. 'Up until a few years ago he fooled around with fraudulent cheques, money with menaces. Then he stopped, for four years. Next time the police heard of him he was into another league entirely.'

'Which was?'

'Gold smuggling.'

Tahlvik looked sharply across at the policeman. 'Using his 'plane?'

Schmidt nodded. 'In the Persian Gulf and Indian Ocean. Flying from India to Dubai. I recall there is a big trade in that part of the world, especially by sea. Big-time operators bring it across and transfer it a few miles off shore into dhows. The authorities then have to look for an Arab boat which looks low in the water. The chances are it is prime full of gold bullion.

'What happened to Rawlings?'

'He landed in the desert. They were waiting for him.'

'What happened?'

Schmidt milked the suspense for as long as he dared. 'He was arrested, charged with illegally importing gold and placed in custody. Then a week later, the charges were dropped.'

Tahlvik stopped walking and looked hard at the lined, mournful face of the Inspector. 'Why?'

'I don't know.'

'Why do you think they were dropped?'

'One explanation could be Rawlings was innocent.'

'Come on, Schmidt,' Tahlvik said. 'You catch a man in the middle of the desert with an aeroplane. You charge him with gold smuggling. That means, surely, they found gold in the 'plane. Couldn't be simpler.'

'That was what I thought.'

'All right, I'll ask you again,' Tahlvik said patiently. 'Why do you think they dropped the charges?'

'On the rare occasions,' Schmidt replied, 'that I have agreed to drop charges, it is because I have gained something in return.'

'Evidence.'

'Or assistance.'

Tahlvik said nothing for half a minute. They stood beside the police helicopter, hands stuck deep into the pockets of their topcoats.

Finally Tahlvik looked at Schmidt. 'Who investigates gold smuggling in the Persian Gulf?' he asked.

Schmidt came to the high point of his performance. 'The British,' he answered.

Tahlvik thanked Schmidt. They walked back to the main gates where they shook hands before Tahlvik climbed into his car and drove back to the Control Tower. He parked below the Tower and hurried across to the entrance.

Suddenly, he stopped. The large black car with the Union Jack on the radiator was still in the line of vehicles that had been there all day. A driver sat behind the steering wheel asleep.

Tahlvik changed direction and marched over to stand by the window beside the driving seat. Raising a knuckle he rattled on it. The driver woke up with a start. He saw Tahlvik and rolled the window down.

'You are who?' Tahlvik demanded.

The driver straightened up and adjusted his peaked hat. 'British Embassy, sir,' he said quickly.

Tahlvik yanked open the car door. 'Out.'

The driver struggled out of the seat in confusion. 'Papers.' Tahlvik held out a hand while the man fumbled inside his coat. It crossed his mind to ask on what authority this man was acting but glancing at the angry, dangerous expression on his face, he chose the line of least resistance and passed over the documents to say he was a registered driver with the British Embassy in Oslo and had permission to park his vehicle on the tarmac of the airport.

Tahlvik flicked through the papers. 'What are you doing here?' he snapped.

'Waiting for the diplomatic mail, sir.'

'Where is it?' The driver pointed in the direction of the hi-jacked Boeing.

'On that 'plane, sir,' he replied.

'Who has it?'

'Queen's Messenger, sir.' To show he had nothing to hide the driver hopped round to the trunk of the car and raised the lid. Inside were a dozen grey hessian bags tied at the top with a large label protruding from the knot which read 'LONDON'.

'He drops incoming mail and picks up outgoing,' the driver said. 'These.'

'Mail to and from the British Embassy?'

'Yes, sir.'

'Where do you exchange them?' Tahlvik asked, pointing to the bags.

'On the tarmac as a rule,' the driver said. 'Mostly the

Messenger doesn't leave the aircraft. He's usually going on with it elsewhere. He drops them down to me. I hand these up. This time though – well, the usual arrangements have gone to cock, haven't they?'

Tahlvik picked one of the bags out of the trunk and weighed it in his hand. It was bulky with packets of mail and books.

'After you have collected the incoming mail, what then?'

'I drive it straight off, back to the Embassy,' the driver said. 'Missing Customs.'

'Yes, sir. It's the rules,' he added quickly.

Tahlvik nodded thoughtfully and dropped the bag back into the trunk.

'All right,' he said.

'Any news about the 'plane, sir,' the driver asked, closing the lid of the trunk. Tahlvik shook his head. He walked away five yards before turning round. 'What is the name of the Queen's Messenger aboard?'

'Brigadier Phillips, sir.'

Tahlvik strode towards the entrance of the Tower. His pace quickened until he was almost running by the time he reached the doors. When Bernhard stepped in his path, coming out from behind the entrance door, Tahlvik almost bowled him over. 'Don't stop me now,' Tahlvik said, dodging round him and jumping into the lift. 'Please.'

The last word came out almost as a plea. Bernhard followed him into the lift, narrowly missing the closing doors as Tahlvik punched a button. They went up one and a half floors before Bernhard pressed the emergency stop button. They came to a jangling stop.

'Now you *have* to listen,' Bernhard said, placing his back against the buttons. Tahlvik looked at his watch.

'In 35 minutes exactly,' he said, 'the 'plane is due to explode.'

'Precisely, Colonel,' Bernhard said. 'You have spent over five hours ignoring orders. As a result you are within half an hour of the deadline. You have come very near to disaster once with that ridiculous escapade, sending a man to try and get aboard. You have tested their patience, chasing off their look-out pilot – what good has that done, might I ask?'

'More than you will appreciate, Bernhard,' Tahlvik said quietly. He wondered what the repercussions would be if he planted a fist into the man's solar plexus.

'Well, if I don't appreciate it, Tahlvik, I'm pretty sure the Government won't either. This *Boy's Own* comic approach has got to stop and stop now. You were given clear and un-ambiguous orders. You chose to act against them. I could already have you suspended from duty.'

'I am here in my capacity of Head of Security,' Tahlvik said, fighting down the anger which rose inside him. 'That does not mean the security of your backside in the Ministry.'

'Unless you release the men from the British Ambassador's house at once, I intend to relieve you of command.'

Tahlvik gave a short, sharp laugh, an expression he didn't feel. 'Where have you been for the last half hour?' he said.

'Trying to get hold of you.'

'I ordered their release over thirty minutes ago,' he said. 'They should be here shortly.'.

The news rocked Bernhard. His first reaction was that it was another of Tahlvik's tricks to gain time. But there was nothing he could do about it standing in a lift stuck between floors. Tahlvik put out a hand and reached a button, pressed it and they climbed the remainder of the distance to the Control Room without speaking.

CHAPTER TWENTY-TWO

'Hello Petrie, this is Sunflower, come in.'

'Hello Sunflower, Petrie here. Where are you?'

'On the way. What is your situation?'

'Cool as ice, brother. New set of wheels, a full tank of fuel. We're waiting for you.'

The motor cyclists ahead of the minibus carved their way through the sparse traffic. The cavalcade caused a few heads to turn but only raised a mild interest. Two police riders cruised a quarter of a mile behind to keep back the squad of following journalists.

Inside the minibus Palmer winced as a spasm passed across his chest, taking his breath away. The pains were now coming at fifteen minute intervals and each one felt worse than the last. The temptation was to swallow another couple of pills to kill the pain but he knew that would merely replace pain with the numbness of death.

Shepherd watched him anxiously. 'Are you all right?' he asked.

Palmer nodded. He even tried a smile. Anything to avoid giving the impression he was trading on his heart to curry sympathy. He recalled the time thirty years earlier when the Gestapo had caught him. He would not then have bet on his ability to refuse a way to kill himself. They hadn't held him just for two days. For five months he had not seen daylight nor, except for his torturers, another human being. Kept alive on bread and goat's milk in a stinking cell in Ljubliana. Years later he had journeyed through Yugoslavia and for some perverse reason bought a loaf of bread and a litre of goat's milk. He had found a cave which curved fifty feet into the hillside so that the daylight didn't penetrate to the back. There he had sat in the darkness, tearing off lumps of bread and swilling them down with the milk. He concentrated hard on the things they had done to him, the electrodes, the extraction of his finger and toenails. He remembered the daily newscasts brought to him; how Tito had been killed and his partisans rounded up; how Churchill had come to terms with Hitler so that the war was ended but prisoners on both sides had been abandoned. He was told his father had been killed in a car smash.

There he had sat, ten years afterwards, trying to recreate hell. The aftertaste of the goat's milk helped but he didn't succeed any more than he had done after the war in England. It seemed another world, another existence. It was almost as if someone else had told him about the experience. The element missing was the thought that at any moment he would die. The cell door could open any time and a German soldier could enter, cock his revolver, tell him that they were tired of trying to make him talk, that they had caught someone else who had told them what they were seeking. And his life would end as a bullet pierced his brain. Looking back he knew he would never have killed himself had he been given a chance. Pain has no memory. When it is gone, life continues pretty much as before. That was why he failed to recreate the terror of those months. Perhaps the only way to do it successfully would be to play Russian roulette. That would provide the missing ingredient.

Missing, that is, until the last two days. For Palmer, as he jogged about under the barrel of Shepherd's gun inside the minibus, now felt again the fear of death. Not from the gun. The threat of a bullet in the brain was now far less frightening than the thought of a small valve to the left of his heart. If that stopped opening, the result would be the same. He knew he had to die and die sooner than most people. But not in the back of a van without his wife, without anyone he knew. Put at its most sentimental, he thought, he wanted to say goodbye and thanks.

Shepherd continued to look anxiously across at Palmer. His

face was a grey-white colour and even in the fading afternoon light, anyone could see he was desperately ill. He was embarrassed when Palmer opened his eyes unexpectedly and caught him staring through the holes of the mask.

'It won't look good if you have to carry me aboard,' Palmer said. 'They might think I am dead, and where will that leave you? I expect that is what is worrying you.'

'No,' Shepherd replied.

'You look worried. Even your mask cannot disguise the fact.'

'You forget I have about a hundred passengers on board the 'plane with which to negotiate our release,' Shepherd said.

Palmer blinked. Yes, he had forgotten. 'Hostages are not the problem.'

'Then what is it?'

Shepherd allowed a short, audible chuckle. 'I'm concerned for your health, Mr Palmer. You are a brave man. You represent authority but that doesn't bother me. You cannot choose too freely in your society the profession you must follow. I shouldn't like to think we have aggravated your illness.'

'Thank you,' Palmer replied softly. Another pain was building up in his chest. Every five minutes now. 'I believe you.'

The radio set in Shepherd's hands crackled. 'Hello, Sunflower, where are you? This is Petrie, Sunflower. State your position.'

Shepherd leaned forwards and poked the driver's shoulder. 'How much farther?' he demanded.

'Five miles,' the driver said.

'Hello, Petrie. We're about five miles away. No traffic on the road, we're making good time. Stand by. Keep this channel open.'

'Roger. Out.'

Shepherd snapped up the speaker switch and fell silent as he looked forwards out of the windscreen in front.

The motor cyclists rattled ahead five feet apart. Their job was simple now they were out of the city. Occasionally they moved out to pass a truck, drawing the minibus with them. They approached an intersection with a feed road. A heavy truck was speeding along the feed road and entered the main highway a hundred yards in front of them. The motor cyclists gunned their machines to warn the driver they wanted to pass but pulled back when they saw that the road passed through a hillside a few hundred yards ahead of the truck.

This was the tunnel Tahlvik and Barnes had passed through earlier that day. The police were familiar with it and knew it was narrow. To pass a truck of the size of the one in front inside the tunnel would be extremely dangerous. On the other hand the truck driver had seen the police and slowed down to a crawl.

One of them turned to the minibus and flapped an arm telling the driver to slow down. Then he accelerated and drew alongside the driver's cabin. Shouting and waving his arm, truck and motor cyclist entered the tunnel with the minibus and second cyclist fifty yards behind.

The driver looked down at the gesticulating policeman and frowned. He raised both hands from the wheel as if to say, 'What have I done wrong?' His nervousness caused him to ram an elbow against the huge steering wheel and the truck suddenly veered sharply towards the side of the tunnel. The driver snatched the controls, over-compensated for the swerve and the truck went into a skid which made the trailer jack-knife against the cabin section. The motor cyclist raced on and just managed to clear the backlash of the trailer. Jamming on all brakes, the driver swung on the wheel and the windscreen in front of him came to rest a yard from the stone wall of the tunnel.

The trailer spun across the road, the end clipping the wall on the other side of the road, then stopped. The minibus entered the tunnel. The driver switched on his lights, then stood on the brakes when he saw the huge barrier across his path. Everyone inside was thrown forwards, Shepherd falling across Palmer, and Terry struck the windscreen with a crack.

The second motor cyclist swung his machine across the road and left a millimetre of rubber from his wheels on the road.

Shepherd was the first to recover. He pushed himself back in his seat and held his gun barrel hard against Palmer's head. 'All right, stay still!' he yelled. 'Nobody move!'

The policeman jumped off his machine and ran round to the driver's cabin. He climbed on to the running board and forced open the door. The driver slumped out, blood coursing down his temple, falling over the shoulder of the policeman who gently brought him down to the ground. By now Terry had jumped out of the passenger seat of the minibus and was brandishing his gun in the policeman's face. 'Get that truck out of the way!' he shouted.

The policeman looked up at him, then pointed to the unconscious driver. 'Wait a minute,' he said, 'this man's seriously hurt!'

'Get it out of the way!' Terry screamed. 'I don't care who's hurt! Move it!'

He ran back to the minibus where Shepherd was trying to call Petrie but the radio gave nothing but a fierce crackling.

'Forget it,' Mike said. 'We're in a tunnel.'

Shepherd slammed the set on the seat next to him. He looked round. The end of the tunnel was a hundred yards away and several cars were stopping behind them.

'Petrie's going to wonder where we've got to,' he muttered.

They watched the police motor cyclist stagger past under the weight of the semi-conscious driver.

As they passed the minibus the policeman leaned close to the driver and whispered in his ear. 'They've bought it,' he said. 'Nice bit of driving.'

'This red paint is dripping in my mouth,' the driver whispered back. 'It tastes like poison.'

The policeman helped him into a car at the rear full of police. 'What's happening?' one of them asked.

'We have to shift the truck,' the cyclist said. 'And we have to take not less than fifteen minutes.'

The police got out and walked slowly forward. One stayed back to hold up the traffic behind.

On the other side of the jack-knifed truck Colonel Donner waved a torch. Farther up the tunnel a second black minibus roared into life and shot out of a layby towards the far exit. He watched it go, squinting at his watch. 'Twenty seconds,' he muttered. 'Not bad.'

The second minibus raced out into the daylight.

Inside, four of Donner's commandos struggled into stocking masks while two elderly men and a middle-aged woman settled into the positions occupied by Shepherd's group and their hostages. One of the men held a two-way radio set which crackled loudly until they cleared the tunnel exit. The interference was replaced by Petrie anxiously calling through: 'Sunflower, hello, Sunflower come in, we lost you –'

'Petrie,' the commando said curtly. 'Sunflower. Went through a tunnel. Everything fine now.'

For several seconds Petrie didn't reply and the men in the vehicle held their breath. 'Roger, Sunflower, hear you O.K. now. In you come.'

The relief was audible. Shepherd's substitute looked through the window. The sun was low on the horizon but the clouds had cleared in the west. 'We're still going to have light when we get there,' he said.

'With these things over our faces, they aren't likely to spot the difference,' another replied. 'We drive up to the escalator and rush them. They won't have time to work it out.'

Behind them the police began to swarm over the truck, making a great deal of noise and shouting to each other. Shepherd held his gun steady against Palmer's head while Terry stood outside the minibus and watched helplessly as the man ahead tried to move the monster out of the way.

CHAPTER TWENTY-THREE

Tahlvik heard the message from the commando to Petrie as the replacement minibus emerged from the tunnel.

So did Bernhard. They stood side by side in the Control Room. 'Thank God,' Bernhard said. 'It sounded as if something had gone wrong.'

Tahlvik's features remained motionless. Well done, Donner, he thought. Now it's up to your men. Damn the weather. The skies clear just when you need darkness. He glanced up at the clock. 5.13. Below the Tower the Press stirred into life after hours of idleness, rubbing their fingers to restore the circulation. The men with the cameras began to form a line on either side of the tarmac where the minibus was expected to pass on its way to the Boeing. They will have some copy to file by the end of the day, Tahlvik thought as he watched them jostle for position. Newspaper headlines formed in his mind. Six-inch-high lettering: 'HIJACK FOILED IN BRILLIANT OPERATION!' Or, and despite himself, the alternative remained more vivid: 'MASSACRE AT AIRPORT – HUNDREDS KILLED!' Either way, the news in less than one hour's time was not going to be about the price of fish.

A telephone buzzed and Matson picked it up. He spoke quickly, quietly into it, replaced the receiver and called across: 'They've just passed through the main gates, Colonel.'

Tahlvik picked up the binoculars. Bernhard moved round the room to look in the direction of the airport road. Dead silence fell.

'Here they come,' Bernhard said.

The minibus threaded a path through the buildings until it reached the edge of the tarmac. There it slowed. The press corps moved forwards and several police ran in front of them waving their arms and telling them to stand clear. Bernhard returned to stand next to Tahlvik as the minibus drove slowly across their vision.

Bernhard glanced at the clock. 5.21. 'You cut it fine, Tahlvik,' he breathed.

Tahlvik made no reply. Bernhard looked at him. He saw Tahlvik's hands gripping the binoculars tightly in front of his chest. His eyes stared without blinking and his jaw was set hard, his teeth visible between parted lips.

Bernhard frowned and looked down at the minibus. The figures inside were unidentifiable, a huddled silhouette against the windows. Something stirred in Bernhard's brain and he snatched the binoculars from Tahlvik and put them to his eyes. He followed the retreating minibus for a second. He wasn't sure, but – 'Matson,' Tahlvik snapped, 'get through to Denver.'

Matson pressed down the microphone switch but before he could speak, Bernhard pointed down at the minibus.

'They've been switched!' he yelled.

Turning, he saw Matson look up with alarm and place a hand belatedly over the top of the microphone. Bernhard caught his breath when he saw Matson try and cut the connection off with the aircraft. Tahlvik swore and his arm came up to punch Bernhard but he checked the movement when Petrie's voice crackled over the set lying on the counter: 'Hello, Sunflower. Pull up right there.'

Tahlvik snatched his head round to look at the minibus. Forty yards still separated it from the Boeing.

'Say that again, Ray,' the commando's voice replied.

'You heard me, Sunflower!' Petrie snapped. 'Stop right there!'

The minibus jerked to a halt. 'Satisfied, Bernhard?' Tahlvik whispered. Bernhard said nothing. His jaw worked furiously as he gnawed on the skin inside his cheek, a trademark of guilt he had displayed all his life.

Matson uncovered the microphone and spoke into it: 'Hello, Captain. Captain Denver – '

Three seconds ticked by.

'Who is the bloody idiot in that Tower?' Denver's voice came on.

'What is happening?' Matson asked.

'You were lucky,' Denver answered. 'Petrie had just left the cabin.'

'Where is he?'

'By the door.'

'Why has he told them to stop?'

'I didn't know he had. I'm stuck in this cabin.'

The radio set crackled into life. 'All right, Sunflower,' Petrie's voice ordered. 'Get out and walk the rest of the way.'

There was no response from the minibus.

'You read me, Sunflower?' Finally: 'Roger, Petrie. Here we come.'

In the fast fading light, Tahlvik watched the minibus a hundred yards away. The doors opened and the occupants stepped down. The people playing the hostages acted convincingly. The others helped them down and they moved slowly across the tarmac towards the 'plane.

The door of the Boeing swung back and two figures stood on either side of the opening. Tahlvik saw one of them bend and throw out the collapsible ladder which snaked down to the concrete.

Then Petrie, his hand on his gun, stepped out of the passenger area and stood on the top rung. He was peering through the gloom at the advancing group. When they were twenty yards away he held up a hand: 'Hold it right there!' he shouted.

The commandos shuffled to a halt. They kept their heads down, pretending to huddle against the cold. A long moment passed.

Then Petrie called out: 'Which one of you is Eva?'

The commandos stood stock still; it was a fatal pause. Petrie waited another two seconds and then threw himself back into the aircraft. He and Joe scrabbled for the door handles. The lead commando snatched at his waistband behind his back and withdrew a revolver. Already he was running towards the escalator. The three 'hostages' broke and scattered as the four commandos hurled themselves forwards. The first jumped on to the escalator before Joe had time to haul it in and by the time he had reached the doorway, two others were climbing the rungs behind him.

The leading commando jumped inside the passenger cabin and held out his revolver, arms stretched, pointing it at Petrie's head.

'Freeze!' he yelled.

The other three raced up behind him and each took a target. Joe, Pete and Petrie stood petrified facing the guns of three commandos, their own weapons half-drawn.

The leading commando looked round. Where was the fourth hi-jacker?

There was a movement between the separation of First Class and Economy sections. Bert appeared. He was holding his gun barrel against the neck of Ann the chief stewardess.

'She gets it first!' he yelled.

The commandos didn't move but their guns wavered.

In the Control Room Tahlvik saw the men rush the 'plane, disappear inside and then heard nothing for half a minute. He strode across to the radio control microphone. 'Denver, it's Tahlvik. What the hell has happened?'

'Your men have got three of them covered,' Denver's terse voice came through. 'The other one has got a gun on my stewardess.'

Tahlvik thumped the table in frustration. 'Who wins, Denver?' he asked.

'You do,' Denver replied cryptically. 'That is, if you are prepared to write off the girl.'

Everyone in the Control Room looked towards Tahlvik and nobody spoke. Hardly anyone breathed.

Tahlvik was unaware of anyone else in the room. Ninety-five

lives saved. One lost. The campaign would be won with a minimum loss. Nobody would blame him. There might even be a chance that they wouldn't kill her, or that the man holding her would be hit before he could fire. The hi-jack would be defeated and his country would not be used in the future for such operations. His point would have been firmly established. For the price of one life.

He glanced at Bernhard but the civil servant was saying nothing. He recalled his earlier remark about the situation not having an acceptable level of casualties. He was right.

'Denver,' Tahlvik said, his voice hardly above a whisper.

'Yes, Colonel.'

'Can you put me through on the intercom?'

'Hold on – ' There was a click at the other end.

'You're through, Colonel.'

In the passenger area the participants in the battle had not moved. It was as if they were carved in stone. The Queen's Messenger, the only passenger remaining in the First Class cabin stared at the drama in front of him without expression, his hands still resting over the diplomatic pouches spread on the seats around him.

Then Tahlvik's voice came over the loudspeaker, clipped, metallic: 'This is Colonel Tahlvik,' he said. 'My men will withdraw.'

The leading commando blinked in surprise. For a second he toyed with the idea of winging the man holding the stewardess. Three inches of his right shoulder protruded. A careful shot at three yards couldn't miss. The blow would make him drop the gun, show himself enough to hit again. The other three were easy. The man who had lowered the escalator looked scared stiff and didn't carry a gun. It would be easy –

'I repeat,' Tahlvik's voice came over again. 'My men will withdraw.'

Very slowly the commandos backed off, holding their guns rigidly on their targets. Feeling their way through the door they descended the escalator backwards.

Tahlvik saw them come out. They backed towards the minibus as someone aboard the Boeing slammed the door shut. He left the radio control microphone and walked slowly over to the two-way set.

He switched it on. 'Donner? This is Tahlvik. It didn't work. Bring them in. No tricks this time.'

He slammed down the set and walked quickly out of the Control Room.

CHAPTER TWENTY-FOUR

The first of the tired, deadened passengers filed out at 5.45. Darkness had fallen and searchlights were brought in to bathe the aircraft in a harsh grey light. When Shepherd's group arrived, the members were made to stand on one side of the escalator until the passengers inside were ready and standing in the aisle. Throughout, Shepherd had stood close to Palmer but his concern with the Ambassador was no longer as a hostage. The old man stooped with a hand held permanently over his heart. But he refused to be assisted, shrugging off Shepherd's arm as they dismounted from the minibus.

Then they had gone aboard and the passengers began to descend. Tahlvik left the Control Room and returned to his office on the floor below. He called Polson but the General was out of reach. Tahlvik left a message for him to call back as soon as possible. He put the telephone down and looked out into the dark beyond the window. The idea of watching Shepherd and his gang walk aboard didn't appeal. He left his office to look for Barnes. He found him in the car park.

'Where's Mrs Palmer?' he asked.

'I put her in the VIP lounge,' Barnes replied.

'Where's that?'

Barnes gave him the directions and Tahlvik walked away. Barnes watched him go. He had known the man long enough to hold off saying 'bad luck'. But he felt sorry for him. Sorrier than Tahlvik would ever know.

Mrs Palmer looked round without interest when Tahlvik walked into the private lounge. She was sitting alone, staring out of a window which looked on to the back of the airport. Magazines lay piled up on the tables but she hadn't touched them.

Tahlvik stood beside her for a moment, then sat down in a

chair opposite. He spoke softly, guessing the contents of her mind. 'You know what has happened?' he asked.

She nodded. 'Captain Barnes told me,' she replied, not looking at him.

'Mrs Palmer – ' Slowly she turned to look at him, ' – you asked me to set the men free who were holding your husband. I told you I couldn't do it. If I was to do my job, I couldn't.'

'I wasn't talking about your ability to carry out your job, Colonel,' she answered. 'Your job was to stop those people endangering your country. I knew that. I was asking you to ignore your duty and extend some mercy towards my husband. You had every right to refuse. A soldier's job is to do his duty.'

'Yes, all right.'

Suddenly Tahlvik felt tired, wearier than he could ever remember having felt in his life before. Failure is tiring. Men who have to face a final defeat usually want to do nothing but crawl away and sleep for a week. From the moment he had ordered the commandos off the Boeing, he had not been able to stop the teeming thoughts from punishing his brain. There would be the inevitable inquiry. The careful sifting of evidence to assess the wisdom or otherwise of his conduct throughout the long afternoon. There would be Bernhard, unmalicious, striving to be fair, but eventually damning in his indictment of the events that had occurred. Polson would privately tell him not to worry but publicly would have no option but to walk away from him. Maybe he should have let them shoot the stewardess. Getting them off would have been treated as a success. If that were the price, he had said to himself, screw success.

But now, here, away from the tenseness of the Control Room, seated in comfort and not having to bark out military commands, Tahlvik could not stoically accept the situation. She had told him he was only doing his job but she had made it sound more like an accusation.

'I can't give in just because there is a gun to my head,' he said. 'It's not my nature.'

Mrs Palmer looked at him. This time she smiled. 'But the gun isn't at your head, Colonel Tahlvik,' she replied quietly. 'The gun is at my husband's head.'

Tahlvik stirred uneasily in his chair. Of all the metaphors to pick at this moment, he had to choose the worst possible one. 'Despite what you think,' he muttered, 'I was trying to protect lives, not waste them. I can only thank God that so far no one has been killed.'

As he said it, he felt a thread pull in his mind, sifting over some incident of the afternoon. But his mind was in turmoil and he lost it almost at once. Like the recall of some distant event, brought to mind after years by a sound, a tune, a phrase, but which vanishes for ever in the next instant.

'I have never accused you of wasting lives,' Mrs Palmer replied. 'But you risk them. You risk the lives of other people, Colonel. Oh, I know as a senior officer, you aren't allowed to go charging about with the front platoon. The first over the hill. You are in command and it is important you remain alive. The commanding officer carries a great responsibility, but one compensation is that he is never required to put his own life in the balance. Isn't that so? He can become an armchair general. Gerald spent four years fighting a hand-to-hand war in Yugoslavia. He fought for the freedom of others. Yugoslavia was good propaganda for Britain during the last war, but nobody ever thought of it as the key to the defeat of Germany. Gerald fought with them, he was captured, he was tortured. His heart never recovered from the ordeal. But he *was* a soldier, Colonel. Men like you merely play a game.'

A flat parade of facts, unemotionally delivered, spoken without a hint of accusation. She finished without looking at him. He could have thought of a reply but it would have served no useful purpose.

He stood up, turned and walked steadily towards the door. When he closed it behind him, she was back staring out of the darkened window, seeing nothing but her reflection. Not even seeing that.

He returned to his office. As he walked across the compound beneath the Tower, he tried to recall the spark which had ignited his brain for a second back there with Mrs Palmer. Killed. No one had been killed, that was it. Now why had the phrase seemed so important, so telling when it had been said? Think, Think! Was there a piece of flesh yet sticking to a bone, a piece to peel off, was there any remnant of hope? No one had been killed. Where did that tie up? Someone, somewhere during the last few hours had said something similar. Where? When?

He hurried up to his office and told the guard to let no one in. He sat at his desk and drew out the miniature tape recorder from his breast pocket. For a long while he looked at it, tapping the plastic box with a finger. Was the answer on the tape?

He ran it back, stopped and pressed the play button. He heard Petrie telling him what they were after, the demands for repairs, water. He ran it forwards and picked up the exchanges between Petrie and Shepherd not long after Petrie received his radio.

When had he got the radio set? After the commando had tried coming up from the rear. The radio had been sent out at the same time to keep their attention distracted.

The commando! He could have been shot. Watching from the window, Tahlvik had stood and waited for the execution to take place. But instead, the man had been sent back. In itself that was not so odd. It was in Petrie's interest to avoid outright murder, having neutralised the commando and made their point about their impregnability, why shoot?

He punched the buttons on his machine several times and then stopped when he heard someone say: '. . . loss of life. Is that clear?'

He ran the tape back a little and played it again: '. . . Captain Barnes of the British Embassy. We are negotiating the release of your men with the authorities. But I warn you, they will refuse outright if there is any loss of life. Is – that – clear?'

Barnes had said it! 'It's clear to me,' Petrie's filtered voice continued on the tape, 'but is it clear to Colonel Tahlvik ? You tell him what you just told me.'

Tahlvik stopped the tape. Barnes had emphasised the danger of killing. But so what ? Why shouldn't he ? Petrie was British. Barnes was simply reminding him that the repercussions would be severe should a Nordlandic citizen be murdered during the operation. He played the extract again. There was a hint of urgency in Barnes's voice. Almost anxiety. Not the kind used in a diplomatic exchange. Almost as if –

God damn his weary brain! That was it – that was the thought which had been buzzing around his mind like a mosquito in the night. Now he remembered. During the storming of the aircraft. The four commandos had raced over the ten yard stretch of tarmac, clambered up the steps and managed to get inside and neutralise three of the four hi-jackers. Watching it, he now recalled being amazed at the success of his men. All Petrie had to do was raise the gun in his hand and that would have been that. He remembered how elated he felt for five seconds, thinking that against all the odds, his men had climbed aboard and kept the initiative. When Denver had reported the position with the stewardess, his disappointment had been so great he had forgotten the nagging thought which had worried him when the men disappeared inside the 'plane. He had forgotten saying to himself 'They can't make it! They must be shot!'

Petrie had jeopardised the entire mission by not firing. He hadn't time to choose, to think back to that stage in the planning when someone had said they stood a better chance if they could avoid killing anybody. During that final, insane confrontation such refinements were irrelevant. Yet no one had opened fire.

Tahlvik reached over and switched on the intercom. 'Matson, is Captain Barnes with you ? Ask him to come down.'

He stood and looked out at the searchlit Boeing. The passengers were streaming across the tarmac in a long, straggling line. Voices sounded beyond the door and he strode across to open it. Barnes was arguing with the sentry. He wore his topcoat and fur hat.

'It's all right,' he said to the guard and motioned Barnes to enter. He closed the door and walked slowly back to the window. Barnes grasped the sombre mood in the room and stayed silent. Tahlvik turned and shrugged heavily. The Englishman gave a nervous grin. 'You can't win them all,' he said.

'No, Frank,' Tahlvik said, smiling wearily. 'You can't.'

After a heavy silence: 'Did you want to see me about anything special, Nils ?'

Tahlvik didn't reply.

'Palmer must be in pretty bad shape by now,' Barnes continued, crossing the floor to look out at the scene. 'He looked all in when he came off the minibus.'

'Yes,'

'Nils,' Barnes said, trying to phrase something but having trouble.

'What is it, Frank ?'

'Do you think they would agree, Petrie would agree, to take me instead of Palmer ?'

Tahlvik turned and stared at him. Barnes shuffled nervously.

'I mean, well, one hostage is as good as another. I'm just afraid Palmer's heart won't take much more strain. They took the 'chutes on board. They might still be planning to bale out. That would certainly kill him, the state he's in at present – '

'Frank,' Tahlvik cut in. 'I should think that Shepherd will do anything to get you on board. Anything.'

Barnes blinked and looked confused.

'Can't you guess why ?'

'Er – no.'

'You saw his face,' Tahlvik said. 'He made a mistake and you had a good look at him. You can swear he was here, you can testify in court he was in charge of the kidnapping of the British Ambassador. Didn't you tell me Shepherd had been making fools of the police for years ? Because he never left

143

any evidence, never made a mistake. Well, he made one here. He'll fly out of here but your evidence will catch him in the end. The world is small today, Frank. Nobody stays free. They catch people from London in the middle of the Brazilian jungle. You are the one person who can justify a world-wide hunt for Shepherd. I'm just waiting for him to *insist* you go on board. Simply so he can toss you out at 30,000 feet.'

Barnes said nothing at all. Tahlvik studied him closely.

'I suppose you're right,' Barnes answered, a tremor betraying his nervousness.

'You really hadn't thought about it that way, had you?' Tahlvik said.

'Actually, no.'

'Don't you agree?'

'Yes, I do, it's just – I – well, I hadn't thought it through that far.'

Tahlvik never took his eyes off him. 'Of course,' he said, 'Petrie wouldn't kill you. Would he?'

Barnes shrugged but there was something in the way he glanced at Tahlvik and away again. 'Petrie plays to your rules, doesn't he, Frank?'

'My rules?'

'Yes.' He leaned towards the desk and pressed the play button on his tape recorder.

'. . . I warn you, they will refuse outright if there is any loss of life. Is – that – clear?'

Barnes started as he recognised his own voice. 'What's that?' he asked.

'That was you.'

'No, the recording,' Barnes said, pointing to the machine.

Tahlvik picked it up. 'A memory aid,' he said. 'Quicker than a notebook. And more accurate.'

He pressed the buttons in quick succession and the tape slipped back a foot, then more slowly forwards again: '. . . refuse outright if there is any loss of life. Is – that – clear?'

Tahlvik stopped it. 'What was that, Frank,' he asked mildly. 'A reminder?'

'I've no idea what you mean – ' Barnes began, but Tahlvik wasn't waiting for answers.

'A reminder to your man Petrie. His orders were simple enough. Hi-jack an aircraft, scare the living shit out of innocent people. But he mustn't kill anyone. You kill someone and we might just blast the whole 'plane to pieces. "Nobody must be hurt." Wasn't that it?'

'Nils,' Barnes said, 'I swear I don't know what you're trying to say.'

'I'm not *trying* to say anything, Captain Barnes,' Tahlvik said. His bantering tone vanished and a dangerous edge appeared in his voice. 'I'm saying it clearly and direct.'

He pressed the play button. 'It's clear to me,' Petrie's voice said. 'But is it clear to Colonel Tahlvik – ' Tahlvik stopped the tape and looked up at Barnes.

'It is now. Perfectly clear.'

'Look, Nils – '

'You've no idea what I'm talking about?' Tahlvik said.

'None.'

'You've been straight with me, you haven't kept anything back, you haven't lied?'

'No!' Barnes almost shouted.

Tahlvik leaned forwards with the air of a man about to put Bobby Fischer into checkmate. 'All right,' he said. 'Then answer me one question. Just one.'

Barnes said nothing but he looked as if he knew he had overlooked something.

'Tell me, Frank,' Tahlvik said, 'where was Shepherd's dropping zone? You remember, Marigold. You told me you had found out where it was. It's no secret any more. Where was it located?'

No reply passed Barnes's lips. He sighed, a long, racking breath and turned away.

'You have no idea where they were going to bale out,'

Tahlvik said, keeping his voice calm and level but filling it with contempt. 'All Petrie could deliver to you was a code-name. Marigold.'

'Nils – '

'I know, Frank. You were only obeying orders. The classic response when crimes are committed in the name of the so-called public good. Shepherd meant so much to you that you went this far to catch him. It must have sent you almost mad when it looked like we were going to let him go. Or perhaps it did send you the whole way into madness. Because I don't think you're aware of what you've done. To catch one man you scared a whole 'planeload of innocent people. You forced me to send men out there who were thinking that at any moment they might have their heads blown off. You prolonged the ordeal of Palmer, whose wife is now convinced he won't live much longer. You made a young stewardess go through an experience she will never forget. All for one enemy of the State who has made a fool of you, whose capture has become some sort of obsession. Who we were going to let go.'

Barnes stayed carefully quiet.

'You were going to catch him and kill him,' Tahlvik added.

'He'll stand trial,' Barnes said.

'He'll never leave that 'plane,' Tahlvik said, 'and you, more than anyone else, know it.'

'Why?'

'You said it yourself,' Tahlvik said. 'You saw his face. You can prove he was here. He would have left Nordland but he'd have been caught anywhere he went. Eventually. And you could stand up in court and identify him. This hi-jack wasn't essential. It wasn't even necessary. Unless, of course, the idea was to get rid of him for good.'

'I'm sorry, Nils,' Barnes whispered.

'So am I, Captain Barnes,' he replied, moving to the door. He shook the key from the lock and opened the door. He left the room, locked the door on the outside and handed the key to the guard.

Outside, the passengers were walking through a gauntlet of reporters and flashbulb explosions. Microphones were shoved under their noses and questions in several languages thrown at them. Some answered quickly, shyly. Others, like Major Ferris, knocked the microphones aside and strode on towards the terminal buildings. The television cameras crowded round the mother with the boy who clutched the Snoopy doll tightly to his chest. They asked the boy how he felt and he said fine. They asked if he had been frightened at all. The boy said only once, and that was when a man had tried to beat up one of the hi-jackers. When the journalists became excited and asked which passenger had done this, Major Ferris increased his step. The boy added he liked one of the hi-jackers and had given him one of his toy cars.

Brigadier Phillips had waited until last to leave the aircraft and walked steadily towards the Control Tower, swinging two bundles of diplomatic bags. The driver from the Embassy met him halfway and took the load. They returned to the car and the driver threw the newly arrived bags into the trunk. 'Where to, sir?' he asked, climbing in behind the wheel.

'The Embassy,' Phillips replied. 'We'll put the mail under lock and key. Then on to the Continental Hotel. I'll continue tomorrow.'

The car started up and swung round in a careful U-turn, threading a way through the passengers and newsmen who thronged the area below the Tower. It drove towards the terminal buildings, then dipped down an incline to reach the road which led to the main gates.

As it turned the corner the driver stamped on the brakes. Ahead of them was a line of policemen across the road. Standing in the middle was Tahlvik.

Phillips leaned out of the rear window.

'Brigadier Phillips,' he called to Tahlvik who was coming round to the side of the car. 'I'm a Queen's Messenger carrying diplomatic mail on behalf of Her Majesty's Government.'

Tahlvik reached out and yanked the rear door open. He looked down at the man.

'You, Brigadier,' he said softly, 'are under arrest.'

Phillips struggled out of the back seat and stood up. 'May I remind you,' he said stiffly, 'that I have diplomatic immunity?'

Tahlvik walked round to the trunk and lifted the lid. He pulled out a bag and held it up.

'That privilege ceased the moment you carried one of these aboard a civil aircraft stuffed with guns. You armed those men on that 'plane. This mail doesn't go through the security checks. What happened, Brigadier? You received a telephone call from an old friend, someone you had served with. He appealed to your patriotic spirit, mouthed a few platitudes like the end justifying the means when the safety of the nation is at stake – and persuaded you to fall in with their scheme to get Shepherd.'

'I have no comment at all,' Phillips said. 'Unless you can think of a charge here and now, I demand to be released.'

Tahlvik looked across at the uniformed Inspector. 'I would like a full description of the hi-jackers,' the Inspector said quietly. 'You will be of great assistance.'

'I have no time – ' the Brigadier began.

'It is an offence to withhold information from the police which could contribute towards the solution of a crime,' the Inspector added.

Phillips stopped protesting and after a short reflective pause, returned to the back seat of the car. The Inspector flicked a finger and one of his men ducked in beside the driver.

'Thank you, Inspector,' Tahlvik said. 'He won't leave the country, not for a day or so, I trust.'

'Our methods are painfully slow, Colonel,' the Inspector said. Tahlvik smiled, saluted and hurried back towards the Tower.

CHAPTER TWENTY-FIVE

The housekeeper couple were the last to move away from the Boeing. Two policemen helped them towards an airport van and they climbed painfully into the rear seats and were driven to the first aid room.

Tahlvik watched the vehicle bump over the floodlit tarmac from the windows of the Control Tower. By his side Donner looked on in silence. Over on the other side of the room Bernhard sat avoiding contact with anybody. A technician came in with a tray of coffee in plastic cups but Bernhard shook his head curtly when he was approached. There was an air of utter fatigue among the men and it would have been impossible to decide whether the underlying mood was that of relief or despair. Bernhard certainly looked nothing like a man who had finally triumphed. And had he cared to look directly at Tahlvik, he might have noticed that the colonel was equally not assuming the mantle of the defeated.

Denver's voice cut through on the intercom asking for permission to start up. Matson looked momentarily across at Tahlvik who nodded briefly. Matson conveyed the instructions and within a minute the soft whine of the engines penetrated the soundproofing. Clouds of snow blew up from the ground behind the aircraft and swirled in front of the beams of the searchlights.

Tahlvik had turned to leave the Control Room when Matson signalled to him. Someone was speaking indistinctly over the microphone.

'Someone asking for you, Colonel,' he said.

'Petrie?'

Matson shook his head.

Tahlvik approached the microphone, then spoke: 'Colonel Tahlvik.'

'I am prepared to negotiate a replacement hostage for the Ambassador.' It was Shepherd.

'Why?'

'He is ill,' Shepherd said calmly. 'If you agree, I am prepared to take someone else.'

'It's hardly a question of whether I agree,' Tahlvik said. 'We need to have someone agree to go as a replacement.'

'That is your problem. I've offered to help the Ambassador. Whether you choose to accept my help is entirely up to you.'

'You presumably have a minimum requirement for whoever volunteers to go with you,' Tahlvik said.

'Obviously,' Shepherd half chuckled, 'it must be someone you would hesitate to shoot down.'

'Any suggestions?'

There was a silence. 'Yes,' Shepherd replied finally. 'I will accept Captain Barnes, the British Military Attaché.'

When Tahlvik returned to his office, the guard said the man inside had not tried to get out. Indeed, when Tahlvik entered the room, Barnes was sitting slumped in a chair behind the desk, his hands thrust inside his topcoat pockets. He glanced up, his look changing from guilt to one of curiosity when he saw Tahlvik smile broadly.

'Good news, Frank,' Tahlvik said.

Barnes said nothing but continued to stare at Tahlvik.

'Shepherd wants to swap you for Palmer.'

There was a long pause as Barnes stood up, hands still embedded in his greatcoat. 'Very well,' he said in a clipped, formal way.

Tahlvik watched him turn nervously and look through the windows at the aircraft spotlighted outside, its engines revving noisily. Barnes didn't move until Tahlvik stood close to him. Then he turned his head but didn't speak.

'You bloody fool,' Tahlvik said. He was neither angry nor particularly contemptuous. The words were delivered with a long drawn-out sigh of pity. He felt an overwhelming sorrow for the man standing near him. A man who had won his friendship, which he didn't give freely. A man who for most of his life had conducted himself with honour and courage. A man who was, perhaps momentarily, distracted when someone asked him to make what would prove to be the most crucial decision of his life. He had agreed to support an idea which by all normal standards he would have rejected. This agreement had now ruined his life.

'You did what you were told,' Tahlvik continued. 'You obeyed your orders. Look where it has got you.'

'I didn't know it would end like this,' Barnes whispered. He shook his head slowly from side to side. 'You can believe what you want to believe about me, I won't blame you. I knew more than I told you at the outset, yes. I didn't tell you because I was ordered not to. We were friends but our jobs are such that our commitments to our countries are greater than personal friendship. But the truth is, Nils, I was not consulted on the hi-jack. I didn't even know about it until the flight was airborne. By that time it was too late. What could I have said or done that would have had the slightest effect? The situation was still that four men were holding a hundred civilians at gunpoint. Should I have stood in the middle of that field out there and publicly announced it was all a put-up job? Where would that have got us? What would you have done in my place, Nils?'

'I don't know,' Tahlvik said quietly. 'I would like to think I would not have boxed myself in like you have done. The last hour I have not been able to keep track of the various thoughts running through my mind. Once I realised where the truth probably lay. One of them kept coming back to worry me. Assuming your people want Shepherd dead and rigged this hi-jack to capture him in order to kill him off, I couldn't see what they would do about Palmer. Here is a man, a senior Ambassador in the British Diplomatic Service, someone with a hero's career. It seemed inconceivable that Petrie would kill Shepherd in front of Palmer. He would be straight round to your Prime Minister and tell all. The world would know about it. At first I went along with the idea that Petrie would be the one to suggest a swap. You for Palmer. That way you only had the pilot to worry about and he wouldn't see the "accident" which Shepherd would suffer. You would land, report back that Shepherd had tried to destroy the 'plane in a suicidal struggle and had to be shot. That seemed the perfect end to your plot. Is that anywhere near the truth?'

Barnes didn't speak but didn't have to. His face showed Tahlvik was skating very near to the facts.

'Then, of course, later,' Tahlvik went on, 'it seemed very likely that Shepherd would be the man keen to get you on board. For the reasons you yourself said. You are the only man in the world who could swear it was Shepherd in the Ambassador's house. Because you saw his face. There must have been quite a tussle out there as to who would get on the line first and ask for you. If it comes to a hand-to-hand between Petrie and Shepherd who do you think will win? You must have some thoughts on it, Frank. Your life depends on the outcome.'

Barnes stayed silent. He took his hands from his pockets and began to button up his coat. He reached for his fur hat on the desk but his outstretched hand was knocked away by Tahlvik who picked up the hat and stood squarely in front of him, barring the way. 'Take off your coat,' he said tersely.

'What are you going to do?'

'Take off your coat.'

Barnes unbuttoned the coat and shrugged it off into Tahlvik's arms. Tahlvik put it on and jammed the hat over his head.

The inference sank through to Barnes. 'They'll kill you!' he said.

Tahlvik turned towards the door. Barnes came over and put a hand on his arm. For a moment the two men looked at each other but now they were strangers.

'They'll kill you,' Barnes repeated, more softly.

Tahlvik removed his arm. He switched on the intercom and asked Matson to put him through to the Boeing.

'Yes?' He recognised Shepherd's voice.

'Captain Barnes is coming out,' he said. Without waiting for a reply, he switched the intercom off. He took hold of the box and giving a heave, yanked the wires out from the wall sockets. He raised the box above his head and dashed it on to the floor where it shattered.

There was one more glance at Barnes and then he was gone, slamming the door behind him.

CHAPTER TWENTY-SIX

The jeep bumped towards the Boeing, bounding off the frozen ground, shaking Tahlvik around as he gripped the wheel. Ahead of him the huge machine was emitting a middle-toned, regular whine as the engines ticked over, idling.

He was fifty yards away when the main doors opened and the collapsible escalator dropped out of the inside to the ground. No one showed themselves. Tahlvik parked the vehicle and walked the rest of the way, blinking beneath the brilliant arc lights, his face tucked into the collar of Barnes's coat. He stopped at the foot of the escalator and looked up through the entrance. Still nobody appeared. He waited a moment then began to ascend the escalator steps slowly measuring his tread.

The entrance loomed up around him and then he was inside. The moment his head passed through the door a gun barrel snaked out from one side and rested on his temple. He turned his head to see Petrie. Petrie turned him quickly towards the wall and searched his pockets. Although Petrie had gained a close look at him, he said nothing. As he felt his pockets examined Tahlvik realised that Petrie and Barnes could never have met. He wasn't sure whether this said more for Barnes or less.

Petrie pulled him round and Tahlvik was conscious of other figures coming forward from the passenger area.

'Where's the Ambassador?' Tahlvik said.

'That's not Barnes!' a voice yelled. Tahlvik turned and saw Shepherd, minus his mask, standing in the aisle, his face twisted in anger. He strode forward, tugging a gun from his belt and stood a foot away from Tahlvik.

'Then who is it?' Petrie asked nervously. His gun flicked up and he held the barrel hard against Tahlvik's ribs. Then he answered his own question.

'Tahlvik?'

'Just what do you think you are doing?' Shepherd asked, reining in his anger and speaking almost mildly. 'Where is this going to get you?'

The others came forward and stood round Tahlvik, half of them looking to Petrie for guidance, half towards Shepherd. The gun burned into his side, but Tahlvik managed to look round at the semi-circle of faces with an outward calm, ending with Shepherd.

'I may not get very far, Shepherd,' he said. 'But you aren't going anywhere.'

Shepherd stiffened when he heard his name mentioned. The other members of his group glanced quickly at Tahlvik, their frowns deepening. What was an unarmed man doing aboard the aircraft, the result of a trick, and *threatening* them – ?

'What do you mean?' Shepherd demanded.

Tahlvik looked from him to Petrie, then back again. 'This man didn't come to save you, Shepherd. He came to catch you. Your trusted friend is a policeman.'

A dead silence fell inside the aircraft. Nobody moved for several long seconds. Shepherd transferred his attention slowly from Tahlvik to Petrie who kept his gun tucked into Tahlvik's body.

'What are you saying?' Shepherd asked, his voice hardly above a whisper.

'I'm saying,' Tahlvik said, 'that this man here has worked undercover in your organisation for a couple of years. He reported to his masters that you had a code name for your dropping zone. Marigold. But he couldn't deliver the name of the actual location because, presumably, you didn't tell him. Is that not so?'

Shepherd swung his head once from side to side. His eyes never left Petrie. Both had guns in their hands; Petrie's remained pointing at Tahlvik, Shepherd's drooped to the floor.

'Only five of us knew where Marigold was,' he said. 'The four of us – ' he nodded towards Eva, Terry and Mike – 'and the man due to fly us out from Marigold.'

He paused.

'We were told by Ray the police had caught him and were swarming all over the dropping area.'

'Your man is sitting in complete seclusion,' Tahlvik said, 'waiting for you as you planned. Nobody discovered where Marigold was. That was merely a device to make you dependent upon these people who came to catch you. My country was letting you go free. The British secret services could see their one chance of nailing you go through the window. Barnes told them you were here. He saw your face. But of course, you are aware of that. That is why you wanted Barnes up here. To kill him.'

Tahlvik wasn't sure but thought Shepherd had long since stopped listening. He was staring hard at Petrie, his hand tightening round the butt of his gun which still pointed at the floor.

Suddenly there was a thud from behind them Tahlvik looked up to see Mike topple sideways and crumple to the ground. Behind him Pete came into view holding a blackjack, the thong twisted round his wrist. Mike's body hit the floor with a crunch, a dead weight, but as it fell already Bert and Terry began to grapple with each other.

For a moment Shepherd's attention was diverted behind him. He instinctively reacted when Mike was hit and the twitch cost him his life. Petrie pulled the gun out of Tahlvik's ribs and fired twice at point blank range. Shepherd took the two bullets in the middle of his chest and the force sent him crashing back against the wall of the cabin.

A split second later Petrie crumbled with a hoarse gasp as Tahlvik's elbow rammed into his stomach. Tahlvik brought the edge of his hand down on Petrie's wrist and the gun popped from his grasp. Tahlvik dropped to retrieve the gun and by so doing missed a shot from Eva who had thrown herself sideways into a row of seats several yards back. Tahlvik left the gun where it lay and scrabbled for cover as a second shot shattered the plastic casing around the call buttons on the underside of the luggage rack.

Meanwhile Pete had climbed over Bert and lifted his black-jack to club Terry. Eva fired a third time and Pete was pushed full length along the aisle, a bullet lodged under his collarbone. He lay on the floor screaming in agony as Tahlvik tried to change seats in a desperate attempt to get near the woman who was causing havoc. She had now transferred her attention to the struggling Terry, beginning to get the worst of it from Bert. She leaned full length along the seat and held her gun against Bert's temple, trying to fix it there as his head bobbed about in the struggle. Tahlvik stood and covered the ground between them in two strides. He grasped her wrist, raised it a foot and brought it hard down on the seat rest. She let go of the weapon with a yell of pain which was cut off as Tahlvik yanked on her arm, dragging her from the seats. He dragged her into the aisle and sent her full length down the aisle towards the entrance doors. He retrieved her gun from the floor, reversed it in his hand, raised it and brought the butt hard down on Bert's head. Bert fell on top of Terry who was holding his neck, choking and fighting for breath.

Tahlvik knelt and waited for Eva to make her final move. She picked herself up from the aisle a foot away from Shepherd whose life had oozed away in a river of blood which now pumped slowly from the hole in his chest. She looked at him once, saw his gun on the seat next to his rag doll body and dived for it.

Tahlvik ducked when he saw her but she turned in another direction.

Petrie was trying to stand, gasping for breath and clutching his stomach after Tahlvik's elbow had emptied it of air. He opened his eyes and the last image they received was of Eva's arm coming up to point at them.

'Pig!' she screamed and fired. The bullet ripped clean

through Petrie's neck and left an exit hole three times bigger than the entry. Petrie coughed once and dropped.

Eva had no more time left after firing the shot. Tahlvik came up behind and hit her once with the butt of the revolver above an ear. Her head snapped forwards and she lay still.

Ignoring Terry, Tahlvik stood and strode quickly forward towards the pilot's cabin. The door opened before he reached the flight deck and he stopped, bringing up the gun.

Joe appeared, his hands on his head. 'Don't shoot,' he said. 'Please!'

Denver's head appeared in the doorway behind him. 'It's all right, Colonel,' Denver said. 'He handed his gun over as soon as he heard the shooting.'

He held up an automatic and Tahlvik grinned.

'Who won?' Denver asked, his face reflecting the tension of the last six hours.

'They didn't,' Tahlvik said briefly. 'Where's the Ambassador?'

'They put him at the back.'

Leaving Joe pinned against the side of the cabin, Tahlvik led the way through the bloody carnage in the First Class section. Denver stared at Shepherd, white-faced and dead. At Petrie, whose body moved in its final death throes. At Pete, paralysed and moaning softly, lying across two seats; Eva and Bert unconscious; Terry as beaten as Joe and as frightened by the blood spilled around them.

Tahlvik saw a figure at the back of the Economy section. He reached Palmer and unwound a scarf which had been wrapped around his eyes and mouth. It fell from his face but the features did not change. Palmer's eyes were open but sightless.

He was dead.

An overwhelming tiredness crawled over Tahlvik, sapping the last reserves of energy. He looked down at the expression on the dead face; peaceful, no pain. The look of a man prepared for death and expecting it. Tahlvik rested his weight on the back of the seats alongside Palmer. He closed his eyes. Nothing he could identify ran through his brain. Except Mrs Palmer talking of her husband's wartime exploits, of her quiet but damning accusation that he risked other people's lives, never his own.

Denver watched Tahlvik, then put a hand gently on his arm. 'There was nothing you could have done,' he said. 'He wouldn't have wanted you to have played it any other way.'

Tahlvik nodded but more to stop the well-meant words. He looked once more briefly at the face which had looked so kindly upon him when he had called on the British Embassy in the last two years. Had it not been for the housekeepers, he was convinced Palmer would have told him not to yield to Shepherd. He would have said he would prefer to die than allow this kind of blackmail. He would have made his job so much easier. He would have died and would not have thought about the sacrifice. He would have supported Tahlvik every step along the way of that afternoon. But Tahlvik knew he had been robbed of whatever grim satisfaction could have been achieved from the events of the day. Because he knew, or thought he did, that had he known his actions would cause the death of Gerald Palmer, he would not have pursued them. He had learned something of himself when he pulled his men out, when all that stood between them and victory was the life of one young stewardess. In these brief instants are convictions born which tell us we are doomed to failure in whatever career we choose.

Tahlvik walked slowly back up the aisle, hardly noticing the bodies around him as he pushed his way through to the exit doors. He ducked and stepped down into the biting night air. Denver moved forwards into the cockpit and cut the engines. He sat in his chair, all strength ebbing away. Through the side windows he watched Tahlvik walk away from the aeroplane. The colonel ignored the waiting jeep and continued in an arrow-straight line across the Control Tower to his car. People were rushing out on to the tarmac. Police and troops clustered round him as he left the airfield. Denver saw him jerk a thumb back at the Boeing, then continue on through the crowds to climb into his car.

There was a flash of headlights as the car turned in the distance and then it was gone from sight.

Denver leaned forwards and flicked on the radio microphone.